DARK SECRET
AT TWENTY-FIVE FEET

Written by

TIM WENTZ

PublishAmerica
Baltimore

*Thank you!
I hope you
enjoy the
adventure.
Tim Wentz*

Hardcover 9781627096638
Softcover 9781462698035
PUBLISHED BY PUBLISHAMERICA, LLLP
www.publishamerica.com
Baltimore

Printed in the United States of America

Disclaimer;

This pre-teen novel is fictional. Although the town of Somer Set is real, as it sits above the Mississinewa Reservoir. The names of towns and newspapers mentioned are true and held harmless. These are in fact, a part of Tim's childhood, including the town of Marion, Indiana.

The beauty of the reservoir and nearby communities hold wonderful memories for Tim Wentz..

Any resemblance to actual persons, living or dead, events, towns or locales is entirely coincidental. There are no malicious intentions or any deficient of character, communities, businesses, departments and/or organizations.

The State of Indiana, the State Police, Federal Bureau of Investigations, County Sheriff and deputies, the Department of Natural Resources, the Army Corps of Engineers, The Boy Scouts of America, local Law Officers and any other Officials, including the people of towns and their communities are respectfully mentioned.

CONTENTS

About Tim Wentz

I live in central Indiana with my wonderful wife, Emily. The love for drawing and writing stories since I was a youngster, has always been a favorite past time of mine. Another favorite hobby of mine, is creating and making wood products. I had such a memorial childhood growing up out in the country and spending time on family farms.

My brother, childhood friends and cousins, helped to full fill my adventures - which in turn, played a part in guiding me to write this teenage adventure story.

After graduating from The Institute of Children's Literature in 2010, I wanted to write this children's novel. Dark Secret at Twenty-Five Feet is my first novel, which I started in January of 2009. Although it has been a long process with me while studying writing, holding a full time job and with my family life. Dark Secret was completed with my illustrations in early 2012.

My publication credits are; The Gang Comic Books, Copyright 2005. #VAu 694-055.

A 3rd Grade reader, "Growing Up Bobby Bullfrog," Copyright 2008. ISBN#978-1-436-4251-3.

A financial family book, "Scavengers among us," Copyright 2008. ISBN# 978-0-615-26439-4.

A comic book, "In the Darkness of the Roots," Copyright 2009. ISSN# 1947- 5322.

More books will be published in the future, so again I appreciate your help and want to say,

Thank You.
Take care, go on adventures and keep on reading.

Sincerely,
Tim Wentz

DARK SECRET AT TWENTY-FIVE FEET

CHAPTER ONE
The Steep and Rugged Cliff

The rugged stone walls, towering above the waters stand strong like they have for hundreds of years. The limestone and shale composite border this Indiana reservoir.

Various oak, maple, and pine trees scatter atop these large formations, draping over the cliffs. The pine tree smell always remind me of my grandparents' knotty-pine living room walls.

Among the trees is our little town, named *Summer Set*, which overlooks the long reservoir. Dad had once said, that many years ago, this sleepy town had once sat along the natural river, which is at the bottom of the reservoir. The Army Corp. of Engineers then decided that in order to control flooding along the long river, a reservoir must be created.

So the river town was moved up above the flood plain and a large dam was built to help control flooding of the communities down stream.

I had heard that some people believed that the town's name came from being able to see the beautiful sunsets on the reservoir's western horizon. Although the town's name appeared on maps long before the reservoir was built. The reservoir attracts many people during the summer to boat, fish and swim in its waters. Local kids living nearby finds it to be a fun recreational playground.

The heat of the summer months attracts our close group of friends we call ourselves *The Buddies*. We would either kayak, fish from the bank, and hike or swim along the shore. A lot of times we would come to the cliff when it was hot, to swing off the rope and drop in the cool waters.

As boats pass by and some bank fishermen fish the rocky shoreline, occasionally our laughter could be heard from up above the cliffs. One of The Buddies - Stevie Thomas, swings out on a rope to drop into the refreshing waters, following our laughter and cheering. Then he swims back to the rocky shore, as another takes his or her turn on the rope. Stevie slowly climbs back to the top of the cliff.

To the surface, Darwin Weese clears his nose and pushes his blonde hair out of his eyes. With side strokes to get out of the way of the next Buddy, he hollers up to Jamie Hart. She holds the rope while talking to me. The beautiful twenty-two mile long reservoir, and the warm weather, places a smile on our faces.

Jamie hands me the rope as she flips back her long brown hair and swats at an annoying fly. I make a buzzing sound while touching the back of her hair.

She smacks me, shouting, "Lucas Losure," as I jump back to laugh at the practical joke.

We have come to the cliffs by ourselves, for several years now. Before we all turned nine we were always accompanied by our parents or older siblings.

A fresh warm breeze rises up from the reservoir as I swing out and flip up my legs to dive in backwards. Half way up the rocky cliff, Darwin pauses to applaud the dive he hasn't yet tried himself.

The easiest way to climb back up is over to the right, many yards from where we swing off of the cliff. This route is not too steep or rocky for us. Stevie stands on the edge to look down, and studies the boulders below. Jamie, stands a few feet away, watches me swim to shore and notices that Stevie is acting like he could jump right off. "No, Stevie. Don't do it," pleads Jamie to her young buddy. He just looks at her and smirks defiantly.

"Stevie, it's not safe. Don't jump, just use the rope," Darwin said to our young stubborn friend.

"Alright Darwin, if you say so," replies Stevie. " It looks like I can clear the rocks." He peers over the edge, then takes the rope from Jamie and steps back to start his vault.

"Just hang on tight and run right out and let go at the end of your swing," said Darwin.

"I know how to do it," replies Stevie. Annoyed by any help from others. Stevie ran right off the edge and let go at the end of the swing. He awkwardly dives in fifteen feet below on his face and chest.

"Nice dive, Stevie," shouts Darwin as we chuckle. Our Buddies, have all known each other since birth, or thereafter, we think. We all live in a small neighborhood on the south end of town.

As the water clears from his nose, Stevie says, "That kind of hurt." We all giggle. Stevie is our youngest buddy at nine years old. He tries his best to keep up with the rest of us. The steep and rocky cliff area is our favorite summer place to cool off.

It seems like we're here every hot day. Stevie slowly climbs up the cliff, his wavy brown hair drips water like a full sponge. Jamie takes a turn on the rope, runs to swing out, screaming and drops in feet first. Jamie is my girlfriend or should I say, she is a girl and a friend of mine. Small in size, she can run and hold her ground. She is twelve years old, just like I am. She comes up sputtering and shouts, "Oh No! Mom is going to kill me." Her pretty, but wet long hair shines in the sun light.

Stevie races to the cliff's edge to see what Jamie is yelling about. "What's wrong?" I ask, watching her swim to the rocky shoreline. Her head is down as she starts to sob.

"The necklace.... It's gone!" Jamie feels around her neck and searches down through the water around her. She glances up to us and says, "She let me borrow it."

Stevie watches from above, and shouts, "Maybe you lost it up here," then looks and walks around the base of the large oak tree. "I don't see it here," he said, kicking at some twigs.

"It must be right there where you jumped in," Darwin yells down to Jamie.

Jamie and I cling to some boulders, straining to see anything shining below the water, "I can't see it," she cries. "We have to find it or I will be in big trouble." She holds her hair to the side and look frantically through the water.

"It's probably lying on the bottom. Dad said it's almost twenty-five feet deep just past the boulders. That's why he put the rope here," I reply, pointing at the long limb that stretches out over the reservoir.

"Can we get it back? It's valuable," she says, pleading with her big blue eyes piercing my eyes.

"I could dive down to see if I can find it," I said. I really enjoy helping her out in a tough situation.

"If you can, just be careful Lucas," says Jamie. I need to find it for her. Out of the water and up the path to the cliff I climb, to start the deep dive.

I took the rope and ran right off of the cliff, swinging high and dove straight down like an arrow with a deep breath. Barely causing a wake. The cooler deep waters felt refreshing in the summer heat. Down deep I swam, with the water visibility only five feet, I reached the bottom.

On the silt-covered floor I looked around for the necklace, but then start to run low on air. Over by the wall, I notice a dark opening, like a cave. My black hair flows in front of the mask, as I swish it back with a wave of my hand.

Quickly I look over the area, returning soon to the surface to catch my starving breath.

"Did you get it?" Jamie asks, sitting on a rock, clinching her hands together over her chest.

"I tried...," gasping for air, and coughing, "... to search the floor the best I could."

Jamie said, "What *am* I going to do now?" I could imagine that her mother will be very upset.

Stevie and Darwin crouching down to comfort our friend, looking concerned about how to get Jamie out of this predicament. Over to them I swim and say, "I have an idea. I'll borrow my brother's scuba gear."

"I don't know about that Lucas," replies Darwin, who acts as if he's not sure it's such a good idea.

As I rest on a boulder, I reply, "Remember when I took scuba-diving lessons a year ago?"

"Yes. But you couldn't finish the test due to an ear problem,"

"I did have a problem then, but I still know how to scuba-dive." Certified or not, ear problem or not, I'm doing it.

Our families knew we were good swimmers. We have all swam here for years and they have always told us to be careful. They would always say, "Just be sure to be home at a certain time."

"It's only twenty-five feet deep, and I won't be down long," I reply, "And my ear is just fine. While I was down there, I did see a cave like opening. I want to see what it is."

"You can do it Lucas," Stevie said, patting me on my back and flips his towel over his arm.

"I know, it'll be all right. Let's go home and we'll come back tomorrow at noon. I'll bring the scuba gear and get the necklace back. Okay?" I said, feeling good about diving like I had just finished the diving class yesterday.

From the water, we can hear laughter coming from beyond the cliff, like its coming from the trees. The sounds of the water and the summer breeze couldn't smother the laughter. We look at each other, puzzled. Stevie asks, "Who's that?" The laughter is not recognized.

Did someone overhear our plans? I point up and said, "Let's go see who's up there." We hurry up the cliff to locate the laughter.

No one was around here as we ran down the trail to see if anyone was in the park. There wasn't anyone there either. We look across the trees to see if anyone was hiding among them.

"Who was that?" Asks Jamie. We all shrug our shoulders, not knowing who it could be.

"I don't know. That was strange. I hope no one over heard us." I put my hand on Jamie's shoulder to assure her that everything will be okay. Again I remind everyone to not tell anyone about tomorrow, or about our plans.

"Maybe the laughter carried across the reservoir from a boat," Darwin replies.

"There are a few boats way out there," Stevie said, pointing back over his shoulder.

"Yeah. That's probably it," I said, fearing that someone was watching and did overhear us.

With towels around our necks, we walk on towards town. The pavement is so hot, even Stevie can't go barefooted, who usually does. He walks alongside in the grassy areas.

This summer is special to us because Jamie and I will be going to middle school this coming fall. Our buddies have all attended Park Side elementary school since 1963 and now a few of us are moving on up to the middle school. These hot summer days, we want to just have fun and to remember the good times we all have had together. A block over, we could hear boys' laughter.

Between the houses we could see a group of high school kids playing basketball. It was Tony Watson and his friends. They are a rough group, whom we avoid. "That laughter, was it the laughter we heard?" I said, as we stand listening to their laughter.

"It kind of sounds like it," said Jamie, as we stand together watching from afar.

"I bet it was them," said Stevie, "And they probably did hear our plans."

"No. I don't think so. They probably didn't hear us," Darwin replies.

"I really don't think they did either," I said. "Come on, let's go." I motion to my friends to come on.

Stevie and Darwin start to flip each other with their towels - a few times making contact.

We all laugh as we race along. Soon, Stevie turns down his street, with one last flip at Jamie and laughs. As Stevie turns to run, Jamie was quick to snap her towel on his back.

He laughs and yells from the smack, and trots on saying, "See you clowns tomorrow."

We all laugh in return, and Darwin replies, "Tomorrow, Stevie."

"Remember, don't say a thing," I had to remind Stevie, as he runs on and waves back.

We feel that as we split up to go to different schools, The Buddies might have different friends or interests.

We can't see that happening to us, but I saw it happen to my brother when he moved on up to high school. "Things don't seem to stay the same as it once was," I've heard him say.

At the time, I didn't know what he meant by that, now I think I know. Kind of sad. We 're now at Jamie's street, and she says, "All right guys. See you all at the cliff around noon," Then turns and skips away, only to stop and yell back, "Hey. Are you sure it's okay?"

We turn towards Jamie and I said, " Of course, it's okay." We all giggle and wave goodbye.

As we walk on down our street, Darwin asks, "Aren't you worried about your ear?"

"That was a year ago and my doctor said if I ever get water in my ear again, to use swimmer's ear drops to remove any water." Darwin had a concerned, puzzled look on his face.

I sense that Darwin was afraid of me scuba diving, "It's no problem. I had a severe inter ear problem then, which made me sick and so I had to quit the class," I said and bump my fist on his shoulder.

Darwin smiles and rubs his shoulder. We have been good friends for sometime now and know how to take each other.

There was now a strong smell of hamburgers cooking on someone's grill. "Wow. You smell that?" Darwin asks, and looks around to see who's grilling.

"There, behind your house... see the grill smoke?" I point towards Darwin's house.

"Oh. Dad loves to grill out. You want a burger?" Darwin smiles and smacks me on the back of my head. We laugh and run on up his driveway to the fence. Being competitive, we joust to be first to the grill as we both fell through the side gate.

Almost falling onto his father's muddy shoes, which was next to the gate. His father, Wesley, pauses between burger flips and says, "Whoa, easy does it guys. If you guys are hungry, help yourself." Darwin's father paints for a living and sometimes paints farm buildings and muddy fence rows.

His father is a good neighbor and has played ball with us many times. He is not much larger than us, so guarding him on the basketball was about even. After picking ourselves up, I reply, "Smells great! Thanks."

"There's plenty of burgers here," he said, stacking up burgers, ready to eat, "Have at it."

"Yeah, we're starved." Darwin said and handed me a paper plate. Our family is going out for supper tonight, so one hamburger won't hurt. My thoughts quickly shift to the dive tomorrow, borrowing James's scuba gear, finding the necklace and checking out the dark opening. I'll have to be sure to bring the underwater flashlight.

"Lucas. What are you thinking about?" Darwin asks, and then taking a big bite out of his hamburger.

He knows me so well, I said, "Oh. Just thinking about tomorrow." We grin and wolf down our burgers. Tomorrow is going to be a big day, I just hope everything will go okay.

CHAPTER TWO

The Diving Search

Awaken early to the smell of coffee brewing, I put on shorts and a tee shirt to go have some breakfast. My brother James is leaving early today to go out of town with some friends. I knew that James would never let me use his stuff, so while he is gone, I will just borrow his scuba gear. Ok, so I'm not certified, but I know how to dive. Dad is at work and Mom going to the city to shop. James will be leaving soon and then I'll go out to the garage to get out the scuba gear.

Mother told me to do my chores and that there was leftovers in the fridge for lunch, and to be home by six o'clock for supper. So this will give me time to get set up, dive down, get the necklace and get back home with the gear. Get it all cleaned up and put away without anyone knowing I ever borrowed it. This isn't the first time I have borrowed anything without permission. Yes. I know it's not the right thing to do, but my family doesn't listen or understand me. Sometimes a guy has to do what has to be done.

Oh... and do my chores before Mother gets back home. Darwin is my best friend, but at times I feel that Jamie is my best friend. I feel good helping my friends, but I *really* feel good helping Jamie out. Isn't that silly?

"Lucas! I am leaving now. See you later punk," James shouts from the front door.

"Alright, later." I reply from my bedroom. He is such a jerk. The front door slams shut. As I watch from across my room, I see James hop in his ride. They back out of the drive and go down the road. He will be gone all day at Indiana Beach with his friends.

There should be plenty of time to pull this off to help my friend Jamie. Now is the time. Past the kitchen and down the hall, to the garage door in five seconds flat. There in the corner of the garage, in a large container, is the scuba gear. The single oxygen tank is heavy. I turn the valve on to check the pressure, to see it has 53 pounds of pressure. Just enough for my dive. The regulator, mouth piece and hoses are all here and look new. The mask and snorkel looks fine. And the inflatable life vest, all set to go. I will adjust everything once we get to the water.

Oh, I just about forgot the diver's flashlight. This is a must if there really is a cave down there. But I have to find Jamie's necklace first. The flashlight tests okay, it looks bright. James just used his gear like two weeks ago with his friends at a Logansport gravel pit, so everything should work fine.

It's ten o'clock now, so I'll call my buddies to see if they'll be ready. At Darwin's house, the answering machine picks up. Maybe he will meet us there. Jamie is next.

She is getting ready and will meet me at the corner in half an hour. I called Stevie' house and his dad said Stevie was at the neighbors playing basketball.

Stevie had talked about going swimming there at the cliffs today. He will give him the message that I had called about going to the cliffs.

All right, I hope everyone shows up to help. I would feel better if everyone was there, in case I need help for some reason. Not that I need help diving, I'll just be going down deep to look around. Just so it won't be obvious that I am going scuba-diving, I'll put everything in my back pack and haul it to the cliff on my back. Here is my back pack and I'll pack the scuba-gear inside. It all has to fit inside. Oh Boy! It all fits tight, I hope the zipper doesn't bust. There, all set, no one will notice what I've got here.

It's time to go meet Jamie. Oh No! This is heavy! I need to get the pack on my back while it's on the floor. This can't be so. I can't even get up with this load. "Come on!" Okay, put the back pack up on a chair, and then back up to the pack to strap it on.

"Wow!" This must weigh like 300 pounds. I weigh like 105 pounds, not light for a 12-year-old. In school, we had to strap on a ton of football equipment and run drills in the heat. So I can do this. But I feel like a big weenie. Out the front door I trudge, bumping into the door frame and stepping down to the side walk. I stagger to the driveway, to meet Jamie, who is waiting for me a block down the street. The straps dig into my shoulders... I can't do this. Can't walk a block, and we still have to walk 4 blocks to the cliff. If I still had my red wagon, I could pull this load. "I Know!" I'll use dad's wheelbarrow.

Again fighting to get the pack up into the wheelbarrow. There! Oh good! This is not hard to push at all.

My neighbor, Mrs. Williamson is out trimming her bushes. With her back to me, I'll hurry on by.

I hope she doesn't see me pushing this load, as I try to keep the wheelbarrow under control.

She may mention to Mom that she saw me pushing a wheelbarrow down the sidewalk. People in this town love to talk. In the short distance, there is Jamie standing on the corner. Now feeling better at pushing this wheelbarrow, although I'm starting to sweat.

Jamie now saw me coming and probably wonders why I have the wheelbarrow. "Hey Jamie. I've got the stuff here."

Jamie replies, "I *see*. So much stuff, that you need a wheelbarrow," wearing sunglasses, cut offs, a short sleeve top, flip flops and holding a towel. "We did say at noon, didn't we?"

"Yeah, but I want to have plenty of time to get set up. There's a lot of stuff here."

She glances down at the back pack and smiles. "Is it that heavy?" She asks, walking along side of me as I watch for any traffic coming.

"It weighs a ton," smiling with heavy breathing. "Let's rest here a minute," as I set down the wheelbarrow and rub my hands. "A few more blocks and we're there."

Jamie waves to me to move over. "Let me push this awhile," and takes right over to help.

Her smile alone made me feel better, as she lifts and pushes on. Jamie can run and play tackle football with the best of the boys. She would always be at the top of the pick, when have pick-up games.

We always have a lot of fun together. The summer sun now begins to heat up.

As we arrive at the park, we have just a little further to go. Over on the swings are a few, little kids with some adults. I just don't want someone to know what we're doing and the word gets back home, or I'll be in big trouble.

Noticing that Jamie seems to tire a little, I have to help her. "Here Jamie, I'll help you," grabbing the side of the wheelbarrow and up the hill we trudge. Just pass the trees to our favorite spot, Darwin is sitting by the oak tree, looking out over the reservoir.

He hears us shuffling his way and turns, "Hey guys, I been waiting. You got something there?" A slight breeze coming up from the reservoir, helps to cool my hot body.

"A load which I couldn't carry on my back," I reply, as we sit the wheelbarrow down.

"There's a bass boat just below and they're fishing along the rocks," Darwin points out. Jamie and I step closer to take a peek over the edge.

"I don't know them. They must be visiting," Jamie said. There are many visitors that come to the reservoir every day to boat, fish or swim. From daylight to dark, the water is a busy place.

"We probably better wait until they pass on by," I reply and then start to unpack the load. Darwin helps set out the gear. "You and Jamie can carry the mask, flashlight, hoses, regulator and snorkel. I'll put on the life vest and carry the tank."

Over to the right side we walk and stop to see if the coast is clear. As the bass boat moves on, the fishermen are casting along the shore.

"They won't have much luck right now. The best fishing is in the morning or in the evening," Darwin said. The noon time summer sun is now roasting our bare skins.

"You're right," I said and carefully we walk down the path to the water. Jamie and Darwin follow carefully with their hands full. The rocks are jagged and sharp, some are loose and slide under each step we take.

We know this area so well, we could probably walk it in the dark. Carefully, we look up and down the reservoir, to make sure we are not seen. Sweat now rolling down my forehead, the water will feel great. "I've got to get in to cool off," as I fall on in.

"Yes," replies Jamie as she sets the equipment down at the water's edge. Then she steps and jumps in to get cooled off. Darwin is right behind her and dives in.

Then I climb back out, to get the equipment. "Okay, I'm ready to get going," placing my arms through the tank straps and inflate the vest with a few puffs of air. Darwin and Jamie get the other equipment, which is a great help. With the regulator on and the tank turned on, the pressure looks good.

All of the straps are set and secured. The flashlight is clipped to the harness.

"Lucas, please find the necklace for me," Jamie said, while handing me the mask and snorkel.

"I'm sure I can find it," I said, as the three of us bob in the water, loading up as if I am going on a expedition for the lost Atlantis. "You two wait up above for me and if anyone comes by, don't say a word about what we're doing. Just act natural. Oh, and don't swing off of the cliff, as I'll soon be coming back up in this area."

"Hey you *guys*," shouts Stevie from up above the cliff, "What are you doing down there?" We shield the sun with our hands to see skinny Stevie stands on the edge looking down at us.

"Shush, Stevie. You'll give us away," said Jamie. She then rushes out of the water to go up to meet him. Darwin also steps on out, while swimming over to the spot of where we would go off of the cliff.

I release the air from the vest to start my dive. "Stevie, just wait up there until I come back," as I lower myself down to test the air again.

With the visibility still at about five feet, I feel comfortable breathing and slowly descend to the bottom. I clear my ears, the deeper I go. The depth of about twenty-five feet, seem to come quick as I can now see the reservoir floor. Littered with rocks and covered with gray silt. Some bass scatters in my presence. The broken sun light flashes the floor with each passing surface wave.

In a few gliding passes of searching, the sparkling necklace appears between two rocks. Bingo! I knew I would find it.

Carefully placing the necklace in my pocket and turning my attention to finding the cave opening. The opening is around here... Oh, there it is. My heart pounding with excitement as I get my flashlight ready. The opening about five feet wide and three feet tall, has rough edges and is tapered at the corners. With the flashlight on, I slowly swim into the dark entrance. The dark cavern waters seem to be cooler than the shallow waters.

Small organisms illuminated by the light beam, dance freely in their water world. The dark passage is a little scary as I concentrate on my breathing and try to stay relaxed.

CHAPTER THREE

The Underwater Cave

The flashlight beam broadcasts around the dark walls and ceiling. Then out of nowhere, I'm startled by a dark ghostly sight and let out a muffled scream, which almost blew out my regulator. A large lake catfish, showing no fear, swims right at me. Pushing myself to the side as the large cat, as big as I am, swim slowly past me. The tank struck the cave wall so hard, I was afraid the tank would blow up. I really need to be careful with my brother's equipment.

Suspended motionless, watching the dark blue monster glide on out into the lake. I've heard stories of and seen big cats caught out of the reservoir before. How many other monsters are hiding in here? I notice that the passage starts to rise up at about a 45-degree angle. This is amazing! I have read about cave diving, and always wanted to do this. This is so cool!

As I descend on up into the cave and break through the water surface. Estimated that I probably have swam in about twenty feet. The flashlight's beam now illuminating a dark cool cavern, filled with ledges, boulders, and formations.

The only thing I heard was the slight hissing of the scuba tank, while removing my mask and regulator. I reach behind me to find the valve to turn off the oxygen. Slowly I pan the flashlight, to see where the cave might lead to from here.

Surprised that this cave, with wonderful formations, was right below our feet. Slowly stepping up out of the water, admiring all of the formations. All of these years and I didn't know this beautiful world was just about ten feet below us.

Our 4th grade teacher told us that caves could be anywhere limestone veins are found in the Indiana bedrock. They are usually formed by water trickling through the bedrock. I sit on a rock looking around, intrigued by the cave's beauty. There are different formations of shapes and sizes, all around me. Tangled and twisted tree roots from above, snake down from the ceiling. The cool air lingers an odor of being damp and musty. Although in the air mix, I caught a whiff of a stinky smell, which I couldn't identify.

I need to go back and tell the others of this cave discovery. I turn on the oxygen tank valve and tested the regulator, to find there wasn't much air pressure. Only six pounds of pressure reads on the hand-held dial. "What happened?" I try the valve again and check the regulator, there was something wrong. I release the tank strap to maneuver the tank around to my lap. As I hold the tank just below the water, bubbles rose up from around the valve. At the valve stem was a crack. It must have happened when I bumped into the cave wall.

My fear that six pounds was not enough to get back out safely. And with the tank still leaking, there is probably twenty feet to swim out and then another twenty-five feet up to the surface. Even with my swimming skills, I'm afraid I won't be able to make it. Now I have damaged James's scuba tank, and will have to get it repaired. "Boy, am I ever going to be in trouble."

But that's the least of my worries. I'm stranded in this cave, with no safe way out. Which could be worse? Getting killed by my brother or a slow death in a cave. It's cool in here and hot outside. Our old teacher said that down in a cave, it's like fifty-five degrees year around. Also in Boy Scouts, we learned that during survival training, one needs to keep calm and cool in a bad situation. This is a bad situation, and it's definitely cool in here! Trapped here without oxygen in the tank. I could practice in the water here, to hold my breath for about a minute and a half.

That's about how long it would take me to swim out of here to the surface. But I had practiced doing that in the scouts, and my best time was only about 65 seconds. Good for a 12-year-old, but bad for this situation. It's too risky. "Think." What can I do?

"Think Lucas." Darkness in a cave is kind of spooky, a single flashlight doesn't get it.

In the quietness of the cavern, I can faintly hear Stevie from up above! "Hey," yelling up at the ceiling. Listen close. "Stevie," oh, I forgot that loud noises can cause a cave-in. Listen... No, it sounds like a faint squeaking noise. Is that Stevie up there? I point the flashlight up at the ceiling. There beyond the stalactites, to the right, are brown bats hanging in a group.

They're making the squeaking noise, talking to each other. Also, they're probably trying to keep warm. Our old teacher also taught us about bats. It's a myth that bats like to fly into your hair. Actually, what happens is when someone moves too fast, the bats just happen to fly into you. I have a thought, "Hey! How did you bats get in this cave?"

There must be a way in here other than under the water. "Yes, that's right."

As I hold the flashlight steady on the bats, some new bats flies into the group from a ceiling back side. The light beam faintly covers the ten foot tall ceiling, but it looks like there is a dark area from where the bats flew in from. That could be my way out of here!

Down the wall from the bats, I see many rocks and ledges. A steep ten foot wall, but not impossible to scale. It is possible to carefully climb up there. Not very far to climb, but, with me being wet could cause me to slip. I'll have to leave the scuba gear here and get it later. I must find a way out of here and I can't wait for a rescue team. "Oh Boy! I would *really* be in trouble," But I won't be in trouble if I was dead.

No Lucas! You're a Boy Scout, you can find a way out of here. "You can do it!" I said to the bats. They don't seem to care that I'm even here.

Over to the wall, I'll try to climb up and hang onto the rocks. But holding the flashlight and trying to climb was hard for me. I need to have a helmet light, like cave spelunkers wear when they explore caves.

An idea pops in my head. I'll use one of the straps from the scuba gear. I'll wrap it around the flashlight and place it on top of my head, and secure the straps down under my chin.

There is a Boy Scout knot called a cove hitch, it will keep the light straight and allow me to see where to go. My thick dark hair provides some cushion, as I reposition the flashlight for comfort.

Secured tight, the straps reach around my forehead and down under my chin. The buckle will let me secure the flashlight in position. My Boy Scout Master would be proud of me. To the wall again, stepping up and grabbing handholds, making sure my feet are planted well. A few more feet, and keeping an eye on the bats, I'm almost there.

The bats are mostly quiet, with a few of them flying in and out. As they flutter about in their little group. My left foot slipped off, but my shoulder caught a jutted ledge. I felt the blunt of the ledge on my shoulder, glancing up to make sure the bats aren't disturbed. I know they are not vampire bats, but like friendly brown cave bats.

With myself stabilized, I carefully work my way on up to the top. As I face the dark opening, the light beam lights up a small horizontal passage. The beam can only reach about fifteen feet, showing some small formations and columns. Beyond that is pitch black. Now I know what that stinky smell is. Its bats poop!

Similar to when my hamster cage needs cleaned. "Gross!" A few bats darting past the light beam, dodging my head. Slowly I move on up into the passage, the bats avoiding a collision with me. The passage is only about four feet wide and maybe two feet tall. I trust the bats will show me the way out of here.

On my stomach I crawl, maneuvering around the formations. My head flashlight slides some as I grab it to readjust. The fluttering of bat wings fills my ears. "Please don't bite me!"

Kind of scary. It's a good thing I'm a small kid, because a man could not squeeze through here. Only wearing shorts and still wet from the dive, the 55 to 60 degree temperature in here is very chilly.

But the strong desire to find a way out here, pushes me on. The odor of bat dung gags me. Is it dung or mud I'm crawling through? I could almost vomit. "Breathe Lucas, breathe!" Some of the squeezes are too tight, so I have to back up to go around other formations.

"Ouch," a bat just hit or bit my left ear. I shook and rub my ear, briefly hiding my face in the crease of my arm. "Ooh, That smarts." This can't be happening.

And I was so careful with these flying-mice. I can't tell if it's bleeding, with all the wetness, mud and dung! I hope he didn't have rabies or I'll have a hard time explaining this. In the scouts, we learned that a series of shots will be given. Maybe I could just clean it up and it'll be all right.

The passage now turns left and drops off into darkness. As I reach the end and pause to see what I could see, the pitch black space has a wide-open sound, like a large empty auditorium. To the edge, the drop off is about seven feet from the floor. There are large rocks scattered below.

As I scan the area to see what I could see, to find the best way down to the floor. The flashlight now presses uncomfortably on my head, I'll have to adjust the strap. Many times I have been on wild cave trips with my Boy Scout troop and so this is not scary for me. But, what's scary is not able to get out of here alive.

To the left are some small ledges for me to climb down. I wipe the muck off of my hands onto my shorts, even though they too are a mess. I make sure each step and handhold is firm, as I work my way down. On a large boulder, planting my feet to rest a minute.

As I search from here, there are some ribbon formations and a few large columns. We also learned that to remember which one is stalagmites and which one is stalactites, just remember that stalagmites *might* reach the ceiling and stalactites hang *tight* on the ceiling.

That stalactites drip water and mineral deposits to form the stalagmites from the floor up.

When the two do meet, they make a column. It takes many, many years to make these beautiful formations. As beautiful as it is, I need to get out of here!

I crouch down, then slide on down to the floor. I need to keep tracking the bats to see where they might be coming in from. It looks like the ceiling could be about nine feet high.

There goes a bat fluttering by. Down I look to see where to step, taking a few more steps. Again up at the ceiling to see where they were flying to and from.

The flashlight feels like its rubbing against my skull, very uncomfortable. I remove the strap to rub my scalp, "Oh that feels better." Now the cave gunk is all in my hair. Oh well, now I must focus the light on the flying bats. Their dark brown bodies are hard to follow against the dark cavern background.

A big mistake was made by taking a few more steps without watching. My feet caught an unusual object, dropping me face down to catch myself with my arms and belly. "Oh!" That hurt.

It's a good thing the floor is mushy here. The flashlight goes bouncing and rolling ahead of me several feet. I look to see that the light didn't get knocked out. Luckily I didn't get hurt.

The desire to survive, pushes me on even though I'm chilled to the bone. My right ear is almost as painful as my bitten left ear, due to the cold. And my finger tips are almost frozen.

With the light still on, which is laying a few feet in front of me, I crawl to reach it. I need to see what it was that tripped me up.

CHAPTER FOUR

An Eerie Discovery

The object felt like a bundle of clothes or some blankets, covered with a sheet of plastic. But it wasn't just blankets, it felt solid like. The unusual find startles me, causing me to snap up my legs up in fear. I turn the light back to focus the light on what, the object might have been. I soon discover, to my surprise, that the bundle is some old blankets covered with a plastic sheet.

Why would there be a plastic sheet or even blankets in a cave? I'm *not* the first one to be here. There must be another way into this cave. Maybe years ago, kids had found this cave and it was their hide-a-way. Slowly I scan the blankets and then look away, as if something else was nearby, or someone was watching me. Fear again overcame me. The plastic sheet dabbled in years of bat dung, is stiff and smells bad.

Someone covered the blankets with plastic, knowing bat dung would soon drop. The shape of the bundle looks long and kind of fluffed up, like a rolled out sleeping bag. Curiously, I crawl slowly over to check the bundle. Soon to find an edge and pulled back the plastic to check the blankets. The flashlight caught the glimpse of a dark gruesome leathery face.

In screaming fear, I drop back on my rear in total shock, scared to death. With rapid breathing and profuse sweating. Barely holding the shaking flashlight out in front of me. Unknowingly, I point the flashlight at the bundle as if the flashlight was a gun.

As I try to hold the flashlight steady, I couldn't believe what I had just seen. Something compelled me, to look into the blanket again, I don't know why, but I did. Maybe I didn't believe what I had seen. Slowly pulling back the blanket's edge and then froze to the sight of a mummy. Dry, dark and wrinkled, with the mouth open and eyes closed. My nose caught a whiff of decay, like the time when we found a dead cat in the alley.

The stench of bat dung couldn't hide this smell. Now feeling sick, I blink my eyes to get a clearer look. Dark brown hair scantily covers the head and seems to be a manly style. My shocked reaction flips the blanket back over the gruesome face which I still couldn't believe. It was as if I had seen a mummy in a museum or a scary Halloween mask.

There is some type of history here. Is this a caveman? A murder? A hermit who lived here and died? Nervously I sit with the flashlight on the bundle and trying to get my breathing under control. To the side of the bundle, there is a dark old bag. A bag next to a skeleton, curiosity wants to see what's inside, while the other part wants to get away. Never the less, I pull apart the tethers to open the... "Oh My! What the... Bundles and bundles of money! Stacks of cash!" Keep quiet Lucas! Someone could hear me babbling.

Through the bundles of money, my fingers lightly flick through, they are all twenty and hundred dollar bills! "Wow!" An unbelievable find!

What does this all mean? A money bag with a skeletal mummified person! Something had happened here years ago and Officer Clifford would love to hear about this one. "Oh! I need to get out of here."

Of all my luck! My flashlight is now going dim. "No! Not now!" I held up and shook the flashlight towards the ceiling, it doesn't seem to help. I can't even see the ceiling. "Please... No!" Slowly the dim light beam shrinks to a yellowish glow and then completely vanishes. "Oh No!" Pitch black. I shake and pound the flashlight but it doesn't help. No power, dead as a door nail, just like this person. So dark, I can't even see my hand in front of my face.

Here I sit next to a skeleton in the darkness. Silence, except for the bats fluttering overhead and squeaking. What else could be scarier? Zombies moaning and walking towards me?

Father would go on late evening walks with his flashlight. He would always go alone in the darkness, walking down by the reservoir. He would never let us go with him on his walks. He would say that he needed time to think, always complaining that his job was stressful. I wish I had his trusted flashlight right now.

I try to contain my composure to stay calm and to remember the bats. They know a way in and out of here. As I squint my eyes to look around in the darkness, over in the far right corner, a dim light glows.

Wow! Is this my way out? Could this be it? My eyes blink and strain to see what might show me the way out, the dim glow is all that I can see. Slowly getting on my hands and knees to crawl towards the light. My judgment estimates it to be about forty feet away, although the darkness confuses me.

It could be twenty feet away. Carefully reaching out to crawl along, just so I don't hit my head on a boulder or a column. "Ouch." My knee picked up a pebble. I pause to rub the pain off my muddy knee. On the dim light, I focus to see if any object may block my view, as stalagmites could be all over.

Slowly I crawl and feel the floor, even though the cave gunk squishes through my fingers. A good hot bath will feel real good right now. Carefully I crawl along to keep safe from a possible drop off or any other sort of danger.

Closer now I can see that the dim light is a reflection off of some large boulders in the corner. Between the boulder and the cavern wall, I crawl to see if I can see where the daylight is coming from.

The light is broken up with flashes of fluttering every once in a while. Even closer now, to see that the broken flashes are caused by bat wings, as the bats come and go. This is their way in and out! Now within four feet, I can see that the light is smothered by tangled vines and tree roots.

This is my way out of here! I look over the opening and realize that it is narrow, but I must work my way out of here. The vines and roots can be moved to the side, enough for me to escape.

"Darn it," I said, remembering that I had dropped the flashlight somewhere back by the skeleton. "Stupid," I mumble, this is just something else to be in trouble with my brother With a crouching stance braced against the wall, I pull at the vines and roots. A gap is forced open, wide enough to stick my head in. The tall gap is from the floor up to my head and only about a foot and a half wide at the middle. Draped across the lower half are spider webs who hold some nasty spiders.

The bright sunshine blinds my guarded eyes. With my eyes squinted, I can see outside. Several trees stand nearby, blocking my view of what looks like houses in the far distance. I turn to look back into the darkness, knowing that a skeleton and a bag full of money is in there. I'm sure that even in death, he is begging for me to come back. Someone to save him from being missing and the truth to be known.

But for now, I must get out safely. The mummified skeleton and money bag mystery will have to wait right now. "I will soon be back, Mr. Skeleton," I softly said.

The wild vegetation holds tight as I fight and wiggle my way into the narrow gap. One end of a vine, I use to brush away the spider webs. The rough opening is about two feet thick with the spider webs guarding the entrance. A few bats seem startled as they try to pass by me. I didn't care, being half way out of the cave, and now breathing a sigh of relief. Even if I do get bitten, I'll be glad to face a hundred rabid needle shots just to get out of this cave.

I push aside more vines and roots, and work my body through, my head is now outside. The rebounding vines and roots try to keep me inside.

The skeleton must have been a small framed person, about my size, I'm guessing. Any bigger and they would not fit inside of this cave. I just hope it wasn't a kid, that would be a tragedy. I don't remember any kid being missing years ago. No run-away or missing person that I have heard of. This is a real mystery.

I squint to see if anyone had seen me emerge out of nowhere. The cave and myself can not be discovered right now. This has to be a secret until the time is just right. The need to get the scuba gear back before I get in trouble, is most important right now.

Still working to inch my way out of this gap, I'm almost free! The summer heat feels so good to my popsicle body. So happy to have survived being trapped in the cave, tears of joy flow with a few choking breaths of the fresh air. The bats saved my life!

If it wasn't for them, I would probably become the second skeleton in there. I must get back to my friends who are probably wondering what is taking me so long.

CHAPTER FIVE

Death-pact Wish

I am lucky to be alive! The bats showed me the way out. My feet gets tangled up in the twisted vines and narrow opening, and causes me to tumble out of the cave onto the ground. Suspiciously, I look around to make sure no one has seen me. The temperature changed drastically from chilling to a heat wave. Such a change that causes my eyes to water and fog up.

Up on my feet, to brush off some spider webs and muck. Now, where am I ? Why... This is the town park! The backside of the park! Here are the swings and ball diamond. Behind a tree I stand to see if I'm alone. No one was in the park. Over there, just beyond the park are two older ladies walking and talking. They are heading towards town, and they probably didn't see me, which is a good thing.

Over to the swings I walk, trying not to look suspicious and to get a better look at the opening. I turn to look back, the hillside is hidden by small trees, brush and vines. From here, I can barely see the darkness of the opening. If I didn't know it was there, I would never have found it.

Although one poor soul did find it many years ago. We have played ball here for years, even home run balls have been hit into the brush before. How could anyone not even notice the cave bats, coming and going?

Remember that spot from here, Lucas. "X marks the spot," I said quietly. There is a mystery hidden in there! I must hurry to my buddies, who are waiting for me. They will be so surprised to see me coming up from behind them. A short run around the end of the park, up the hillside trail and through the trees standing on the cliff. The Buddies sit on the edge looking down into the water, expecting me to come up at any time. "Hey Guys," I said.

They turn and gasp, "Lucas!" All in unison they shout and scramble to their feet.

"Where did you come from?" Darwin asks, with his hands and arms out in total surprise.

Stevie rushes to me, asking, "What a magic trick! How did you do that?"

Jamie with her hands on her forehead, said, "We were getting worried. How did you dive down and come up from behind us? You're all muddy and you stink," she said, now holding her nose. They're looking at me up and down, like I had just crawled out of the sewage.

With one hand trying to control Stevie who is excited and my other to hush the loud questions, I reply, "Quiet guys. I'll tell you." Scared that someone had heard them, I look around. Then whisper, "Let's go down by the water, so I can wash off." We rush to climb down the cliff and without hesitation, I jump into the water to wash off the muck.

Stevie is right behind me. Jamie and Darwin sit on a rock in the water, waiting for my explanation.

"Did you find my necklace?" Jamie asks, with a sincere look on her face.

"I did," I said, as I reach into my pocket and pull the necklace out. "It may need to be cleaned up."

"Thank you!" Jamie takes and cleans it off, "You saved me Lucas! I'm so relieved." She places it around her neck with a big grin.

"So you found it right down there and then went into the cave?" She said, seeming to be upset that I went in the cave alone.

As I keep rinsing myself, I reply, "Yes. The opening was right in the same area, so I had to explore it while I had the chance. Listen to me guys, *you* are not going to believe this!"

Before I could start explaining, Jamie scolded me, "We wish you would have told us you were going to go into the cave. We were scared for you, Lucas!"

"Sorry, but the opportunity was right there. I didn't know the oxygen was going to leak out. Just let me explain the whole story." Again glancing all around to make sure we were not over-heard. There is a boat a long way from us, they couldn't possibly hear us. I explain in detail the exciting adventure and what I had found. My buddies thought I was joking and they wanted to go see themselves.

This is going to be difficult. I plead to them, that I could be in big trouble if we didn't keep quiet and that we need to plan this out. They all said all right, but I didn't feel good about this. As I'm washing my face, the clear water around me still cloudy from the cave muck. Stevie giggles while rubbing the muck off of my back.

I wash and check my ear for bleeding, and nothing is seen, but it still stings some with pain. "Can you see if my ear is bleeding?" I ask Jamie. As I lean towards her, for her to get a good look.

She tilts my head and looks close, saying "No, it looks like a scratch and it's a little red."

"Oh, I thought a bat had bitten me, but since it's just a scratch."

"When you get home, I would clean it good with soap and hot water, and then put antibiotic cream on it,"

"I'm glad it's not a bite, I didn't want to get shots for rabies."

"It'll probably be all right," Darwin said, leaning in to get a good look at my ear.

I could just tell by their reaction, that someone or two, may not keep our secret quiet for long. Even though I pleaded with them, and they said they wouldn't tell anyone. Stevie for one, would probably blab to a total stranger. In deep thought, I came up with an idea. "Hey guys. You say you won't say anything about this to anyone, will you?" As I climb up out of the water and sit next to my buddies.

They agree in keeping this a secret. I felt unsure, and said "Okay, then let's make a death-pact wish together."

"A death-pact wish? What is that?" Jamie asks, wiping a smudge of muck off of my arm.

Darwin and Stevie had the same question. They sit even closer to me, to hear of my pact idea.

"We together... the four of us, will agree to not say anything about the scuba-gear, or diving down and finding a cave or about the skeleton or the money. If any one of us, says anything about this to anyone outside of our buddy group, before the time is right, we wish a sudden gruesome death to the one who blabs."

Their mouths and eyes wide open in fear. They seem to be in a daze with many thought. "But we said we wouldn't tell. Why the death-pact wish?" Darwin asks.

"This is to assure no one slips and blabs anything about this. The thought of a sudden tragic death scares us to keep quiet. This will be our summer secret. We can privately talk to each other about this, but no one else, until, we decide the time is right to go to the authorities," I explained.

"I can't even tell my mom?" Stevie asks.

"No. No one but the four of us. This is the buddies secret. You don't want to die an awful death, do you?" I said to Stevie. Stevie lowers and shakes his head 'No' in a scared sorrowful response.

"We can do this guys. I know we can. This will just help us to keep this a true secret among us," Jamie said. She places her hands on the knees of Darwin and Stevie. She gestures for them to understand my death-pact idea. "Don't you guys understand and agree?"

"I don't want to die," Stevie replies, with a concern look on his face.

"Yeah. We don't want to die either, so this pact will help keep us quiet," Darwin replies. I broke a smile and nod to them in agreement.

"Okay then, this is what we'll do. Spit into each of your hands and then we'll hold hands. Then you'll repeat after me." I spit into my hands, and the others follow, spitting into their hands. We took each others hand, sitting in a circle. Expression of gross came across their faces, to the slimy hand holds. "Now repeat after me," and they all repeated,

"I solemnly swear to not tell anyone about the scuba-diving, finding an underwater cave, a skeleton, a money bag or anything related to today's event - or I wish to face a sudden severe gruesome death. Only when the time is right, we will report this to Officer Clifford. So help me God."

The buddies all repeated the death-pact vow together. Darwin and Stevie held their heads low. Jamie and I look at each other. We all let go of each others hand. Stevie wipes his hands on his shorts. Quietly we wash our hands in the water without talking.

Soon, Stevie looks up and asks, "Does that mean that if we do tell anyone, God will kill us?"

We all stop washing and look up to each other. "No Stevie. God doesn't kill. It was a sincere wish we took, asking God to help us keep quiet. But if we do break the wish, something awful will happen," I said, "But not by the power of God."

"Oh yeah. I remember that from Sunday school," Stevie said, "But I do promise not to tell anyone."

As we grin at each other, we all knew that we would keep it a secret. "What will we do next?" Asks Darwin.

"That's a good question," I reply, and scratch my head. We sit around in the water and probably still fearing that we might be over heard of our secret.

"How much money is in the bag?" Stevie asks, jumping right from the pact discussion to the money.

"Shush," I quickly said, "You're too loud." Just as I finish explaining, a large splash explodes just two yards away, startling all of us.

My first thought was a big bass, then Darwin shouts and points up, "Hey! Someone up there threw a big rock." Out of the water and up the side of the cliff we climb as fast as we could.

As Jamie reaches the top first, she points and says, "Lucas! Who is that?"

I guide and now push Stevie on up, to look to where she was pointing. There running down past the park was three older boys. We could faintly hear them laughing. "It looks like Tony Watson and his friends," I reply.

The wheelbarrow was pushed over next to some trees. My back pack laying next to it in the brush. "Oh, those guys!" Darwin said, as we watch them race along the park towards town.

"I know him," said Jamie, standing next to me along with Darwin and Stevie. "He is a few years older than us. He's known to play pranks on people." Jamie flips her hair back in disgust.

"I hope they didn't hear what we were talking about," I reply, as they disappear into town.

"What if they did hear us?" Darwin asks, "Then what?"

"Come on," I said. Over to the edge of the cliff we rush, "Now you and Stevie go back down in the water and talk just like we were talking before. Jamie and I will see if we can hear you talking from up here."

Down the side of the cliff they went, looking up and waving. In the water now, they start talking. Jamie and I listen. With the gentle breeze blowing, we could hear them, but couldn't make out what they were saying, "Are you talking at the same level of voice, that we were talking before?" I said to them.

"Yeah. We think we are," replies Darwin. We wave for them to come back up the cliff.

"I think we're safe," Jamie said, "Tony was just messing with us, that's all."

"Yeah, I guess you're right. I couldn't hear what they were saying." Stevie and Darwin now with us, "All right guys, see how scary this can be."

"We have to remember the pact and if we do talk to each other about this, make sure no one is around and just whisper." I said. They all agree. "Listen, my friends. I have another idea."

Stevie quickly asks, "Am I going to die because I spoke too loud?", with a scared look on his face.

" No Stevie. We think you're safe this time, but just remember to keep quiet. It's very important to keep this a secret. Your life depends on it! When the time is right, we will all together go tell Officer Clifford about our new discovery," I said in a quiet voice. My buddies all came in close to listen to the plan. I explain that the cave's park entrance will be a new discovery and we explored the cave to find the mummy with the money bag. Nothing about the under water entrance.

Yes. When the time is right, we will all report this to Officer Clifford and we won't reveal the real truth about today, and the death-pact we agreed to. We will say nothing about what happened today. Again, the death-pact wish will hold us true and quite. It will be okay. "The scuba gear is still in the cave and we need to get it back home, before it's found missing from the garage. But it's getting late and we better head home for now. We'll come back tomorrow to play in the park and pretend to make a new discovery."

"But we could be rich, Lucas," Stevie replies, again asking about the money, "Can't we just keep some of it?"

"That sounds nice Stevie, but it's not our money. This can cause us a lot of trouble."

"Then they might say we killed this person and hid the body in the cave," Darwin said.

"Yeah. We have to report everything, as we had found it in the park," replies Jamie.

"I guess you're right," Stevie said, disappointed and kicks at some pebbles in the dirt.

"Come on, let's get going," I reply, walking towards the wheelbarrow. I set the wheelbarrow back up-right and toss the back pack in it. Down the trail we went to the park. There was no one in the park right now and I took a quick glance towards the hidden entrance.

"Where is it at, Lucas?" Stevie said in a whisper. He must have sensed it was over there somewhere.

"Tomorrow, I'll show everyone," I said, smiling as we keep on going. "If there ever is the best secret in the whole wide world, this is it! Just remember the death-pact wish." Jamie and Darwin smile and glance on past the ball diamond. Stevie even points.

"Let's not act suspicious, someone might ask you what's going on," I said, informing my buddies, "We have to act natural, like nothing is on our mind."

"Sometimes, nothing is going on in my mind," Stevie said and giggles. We all look at him and bust out laughing.

CHAPTER SIX
Return To The Cave

"Let's meet back here tomorrow at 10:00 a.m.. We'll sneak in the cave and get the scuba gear out. We'll clean it up and get it back in the garage. All without being noticed!

Darwin, can you bring a good flashlight tomorrow?" I ask, "I'll also bring a good one."

"Sure I can. You can count on me," said Darwin and pats my back.

Stevie spoke up, "I can probably bring my older sister's flashlight. She sleeps a lot during the day, because she stays up late at night. She likes to go out at night looking for night crawlers, so she can go cat fishing. Some people say she's a loner, whatever that means."

Stevie rarely spoke of her. I reply, "No, that's okay Stevie. We'll bring ours." We knew Stevie's sister keeps to herself and is kind of weird. Stevie hops in the wheelbarrow, as we push on down the sidewalk. I try to steady it with Stevie hanging on.

A car horn beeps behind us as we turn to look. It was Darwin's Mother. She pulls up beside us and Darwin goes over to the passenger window. They talk some and then, she waves goodbye to all of us. We act like nothing is wrong. We wave back, and she slowly drives away. "What's up?" I ask.

"She was going home from visiting some friends and said that supper will be ready in a few hours." Darwin said.

"Did she ask what we were up to?" Jamie asks.

"No. I just said we were playing around the park with Lucas's wheelbarrow."

"Good job Darwin!" I said, with a smile of relief.

"That was a close one," Stevie says, as he hangs on tight and looks at Jamie.

She hops in the wheelbarrow behind Stevie and puts her arms around him. He playfully screams out. I fight to control the off-balanced load, Darwin helps to balance it as we laugh and head on home.

The next day brings clouds and some rain. I brought back the wheelbarrow, back pack and another good working flashlight. Stevie, Darwin and Jamie is by the swings waiting for me.

"Hey guys. This morning, I had some explaining to do to Mom."

"About what?" Jamie asks, while hanging on the swing.

"She received a call from a friend, who said that she saw me pushing the wheelbarrow down the sidewalk yesterday. I told Mom we were just playing at the cliff. She laughed and told me to be careful. She trusts and knows we are just fine playing at the cliff."

"What about the death pact?" Stevie softly asks.

"It didn't have anything to do with what our pact was about. I didn't say anything about diving down, the skeleton or the money," I explain quietly.

Stevie replies, "Oh, that's right," and pushes himself away on the swing.

Jamie eases over to me and asks, "So where is the cave opening, Lucas?"

"It's right over there in the trees and brush." I whisper and nod over towards the hillside.

"I don't see it," replies Jamie, glancing over to the hillside. Darwin and Stevie looks at us.

"That's good. It's well hidden," I said, while checking that we were not being watched.

"I brought a good flashlight, Lucas," said Darwin.

"Good. Two good flashlights will work best for us in there," I said.

"But I don't feel good about going in there. It can be dangerous, Lucas," replies Darwin.

"I'll go in to help you, Lucas," Stevie said.

"Stevie, you better let me go in with Lucas," Jamie insists.

"Ah... Come on you guys. I can do it," Stevie said. As he stands in front of us.

"You and Darwin stand guard out here. Just hang around and don't look suspicious. If anyone comes around, remember the pact and act natural," I explain.

" If anyone asks about us, say we went to some friends house and we'll be back," I softly said, "We'll take the wheelbarrow over to the cliff trail, so it doesn't look apart of the cave.'

Back at the swings, we made sure no one was around the park. "We'll be back out in 15 to 20 minutes," I said, "Now don't watch us, just play." Over to the cave we sneak. I pull back the vines and roots to climb inside. Carefully I wiggle through and then helped Jamie to work her way in.

"Oh wow, this is wild," Jamie whispers. With her flashlight on, we crawl between the wall and boulder. As I coach her along, we were then able to stand up. Jamie brushes off and adjusts her clothes. "It's really cool in here."

"We're going to be a mess before we get out of here, so don't worry about looking nice," I said. The flashlights guide the way, showing Jamie how neat of a cave this is. She found it to be amazing!

"Wow!" She said, as she slowly scans the area, trying to see everything in the light beam.

"This is cool. I can't believe it's been here all the time and no one ever knew it. It kind of smells like a litter box in here," she said. She looks up and around at all of the beautiful formations. "Bats," She said, following them with her flashlight as they flutter about.

"Yeah. They won't bother us. It's damp and musty, with bat dung everywhere. This is really something, isn't it?" I still find this hard to believe. Over to the plastic sheet, and the bundle we walk, Jamie still admiring the formations. "What do you think of this?" I said, trying to get her attention.

She looks down to see the bundle, as I turn the plastic and the blanket edge back to reveal a dark leathery face. "Gosh, it's scary," her hand over her mouth in disbelief. " I wonder who it could be?" She asks.

"That's a good question, and *why* is there a bag full of money here?"

"Wow! Maybe a river pirate from the old reservoir river and this is his loot!"

"I never thought of that, but I don't think so. Let's get going, we have to get the scuba stuff and get out of here." My flashlight pans over to the right, as we carefully walk on.

Up on some large rocks we climb. "Here, hold my flashlight while I go on up."

Jamie holds the flashlights up the wall, watching me climb. Beyond the lights, bats flutter by.

"Now let me have the flashlights, and then, I'll help pull you on up," on my stomach, I reach out to take them from her.

"Here these are, I can climb up myself," she said, being very confident as she climbs on up while I move out of her way. Through the small passage we crawl, snaking around the formations. "Oh, this is slimy stuff we are crawling through. And it smells bad."

"Mud and bat dung, it's all muck," I said, laughing, "Remember the muddy messes we've been in before?" Many times we have played in creeks and mud puddles. "Just move slowly, so the bats don't fly into you."

"I hope they don't bite me," she said, keeping her head low while crawling along. A few bats flutter past our heads.

"Oh, they're so close." She whines.

"If we move slow, we may not get bit. Jamie, I really appreciate you helping me out." We lay together, side by side in the narrow passage. Her flashlight shines in my face.

She starts to giggle, "What?" I ask. Her face has a reflective light glow from our lights.

"You have dung on your face!" She giggles some more.

I wipe my nose off in my elbow pit, "Oh well. It'll wash off." The thought of it, tickles me. To the edge again and watching the bats, I turn around to descend to the other side to where the scuba gear was left. Carefully down, I start, while she shines the lights my way.

"You stay here and I'll hoist the gear up to you." I said, as I slowly went on down.

"All right. I'll stay still right here."

Down below the scuba gear lays right where I had left it, still damp from yesterday. I struggle to lift the tank up above my head.

Steady as I hold it high above my out stretched arms, "Can you grab it by the valve handle?" I start to shake from the heavy weight, I hope Jamie can grab it.

Jamie moves closer, while grasping a stalagmite with one hand, she stretches down and grasps the handle. "I've got it." She strains to lift it out of my hands.

Slowly the tank goes up, "Hang on tight. Try not to bang it around."

"Gosh. It's heavy!" As the tank slides and grinds up and over the wall, disappearing into the passage. The metal tank pinging and scrapping along, the sound amplifies through the cavern.

"Careful Jamie," I said, concerned of it being damaged, "Just hold it there and I'll be right up."

"I'm being as careful as I can. This tank is awkward and heavy!"

"Okay." The rest of the gear is also here where I left them. With all the gear secured across my shoulders, I start my climb up the rugged wall.

Jamie again, shines her light down to help me see my way, "Are you okay?" She asks.

"Yeah." I slowly climb up to her. In the passage I join her and lay on my side, to rest just a minute, to catch my breath.

The bats are squeaking and fluttering by us. Jamie giggles and says, "We're doing okay."

"Yeah we are. All right, I'm ready," as I turn over to crawl on. "Here, you take this stuff and I'll get the tank."

Jamie takes part of the load, while I bring the tank. As I drag and ping along, "Oh. I can't scrape this tank up, more so than it already is." Now on the other side again, Jamie climbs down and stands on the boulder.

Slowly I lower the tank down to her. She sits it down and steadies it. She again shines the light to where I'm going.

"We're almost out of here," she said, and steps on down while I take the tank again.

We shine our flashlights on the gruesome discovery, as we walk on. Bats still flying about.

"Let's rest here a minute," I said, clanging down the tank and feeling exhausted.

After a few seconds, Jamie said, "You know, we need to report this as soon as we can."

"Yes, I know. But like I said, I don't want to get into trouble. Yeah, I'm taking a big chance on being seen, but this is my best plan."

"Okay. We're all in this together. Come on, let's get out of here." We pick up the gear to walk over to the cave exit.

Sitting the tank down next to the exit. I ask, "Do you want to go out first?"

"Yes, I want to get out of here," she said, as she crouches down to take the scuba gear with her. "I can smell some fresh air now!"

Right behind her, I drag the tank as careful as I can. Jamie pulls and struggles by the heavy vegetation. "Your doing good Jamie! Keep working your way out and be sure no one can see you come out." Being smaller than myself, she goes through fairly quick. Then she stops and backs up, "What's wrong?" I ask.

She sits back down and softly says, "There's some other kids out there with Darwin and Stevie."

"What? Oh no. Who is it?"

"I don't know, couldn't see. And I didn't want to be seen," Jamie said very quietly.

"Okay, let me take a peek." I said, as Jamie crawls to the side, as I crawl on up and slowly struggle through the jungle, just enough to see the swings.

There I can see Darwin sitting on a swing, talking to Tony Watson. Stevie is hanging on the swing set bar, rocking back and forth. Slowly I back up and sit down. "Oh Boy. It's Tony Watson. I wonder what he's up to?"

"What are they talking about?" Jamie whispers.

"I don't know, I can't hear them talking. We're going to have to wait. I hope Darwin gets rid of him soon."

After a few minutes, I check again, slowly working my way through to peek. Tony is still talking to Darwin, who is now standing and acting like he is trying to walk away. He seems to be held up by Tony talking to him. Oh, there's Stevie. He's also walking, now running away. I'd like to know what's going on! Back into the cave, to inform Jamie what I had seen.

"Does it seem like Darwin is trying to get rid of him?" Jamie quietly asks.

"Yeah, it does. But that's not like Tony, to talk to any of us like that. I wonder what's up? Maybe he's gone now." I turn to head back out, crawling through again. Slowly peeking, no one to be seen. Inch-by-inch, worming my way out, I suspiciously look around.

I work my body out slowly, while looking all around. It looks safe! Turn to face the exit, to say, "All clear Jamie, come on out."

The tank can be heard coming out, I reach in to find the handle and pull it on out.

Over to the cliff trail, there is Darwin standing, with Stevie in the wheelbarrow. I didn't want to wave, in fear of Tony being nearby.

Darwin looks and sees me, he starts pushing the wheelbarrow this way. Stevie riding inside hanging on, while being bounced around. I told Jamie that Darwin and Stevie is coming over, and so the coast must be clear.

Jamie pops her head out, Darwin and Stevie coming on over to help. "Gosh! It's good to get back outside," Jamie said. We help to guide her on out with the other equipment.

"What was Tony talking to you about?" I ask Darwin.

Darwin replies, "He came by, just to ask what we we're doing. We said we're just swinging. Then he asks where you were. We said we're waiting for you guys to come back from visiting a friend's house. And also, what was the wheelbarrow over on the trail for?"

"He is asking a lot of questions, and why did he want to know where we're at?" I asked.

"Yeah, that seems strange," Jamie said. As we start placing the scuba gear in the wheelbarrow. I look again to see if anyone was around the park.

"Then he asks if we had any money!" Stevie said, "We told him we didn't have any and we were just pushing each other up and down the trail in the wheelbarrow."

"The bully!" I reply, "We better get out of here. Where did Tony go from here?"

"He went on towards town. Didn't say where he was going," said Darwin.

"You guys did very good. I was afraid he would discover us and the cave. Let's go down to the water to wash up." I said. Along the back of the park, next to the center field fence, we head on towards the cliff trail.

CHAPTER SEVEN

Confrontations

"You two are all yucky and smell like dog do-do," Stevie said while holding his nose.

"Thanks, Stevie. You want some of this on you?" Jamie replies, reaching out to him.

Stevie yells, "NO," and runs towards the trail, trying to keep the wheelbarrow under control.

"We were hoping you guys would get rid of Tony," I said to Darwin and Stevie. Jamie nods.

"I was scared that he would find out what we were up to," Stevie replies, while pushing hard to get the wheelbarrow up the cliff trail. Jamie coaches him to push harder.

"He must have been bored, with his friends not being around" said Darwin. Tony doesn't have many friends and when he does talk to us, he's not nice about it. His so-called friends aren't nice either. Sometimes they get in trouble around town. Officer Clifford has had to talk to them and their parents before.

"I've got to get washed off," Jamie said, reaching the top of the cliff area. She races to the rope, checks below to make sure the water area is clear.

One time last year, she hurried to go off the rope and there was a fishing boat just below. It was scary. Jamie just hung on and swung back to the cliff. It could have been bad for her, and the two guys fishing below. "I'll be next," I said, while watching Jamie swing off of the cliff, far out and dropping below.

She always makes a small squealing noise when she goes off of the cliff. Where us boys might make a grunting noise when we do a difficult dive or flip.

Jamie is out of the way before I rush out to go into a dive. Soon Jamie and I are washing and swimming back to the shore. We rub off the muck as we swim along. The others are following us, swinging off of the cliff, one at a time.

"This is so refreshing!" Jamie said. She washes her hair, while sitting in now cloudy water.

"Oh yes! So good," I reply, "We probably better get the gear down here to wash it off."

"Alright, let's go." I said, as Stevie swims to us as we're getting out. Darwin just now drops in feet first. "We'll be right back down with the scuba gear."

"Okay," Stevie said sputtering. We slowly walk on up to the top. Our old tennis shoes squishing out water with every step, sometimes slipping on the slate and loose flagstone.

I pick up the tank and slowly walk back down, with Jamie right behind with her arms carrying the rest of the gear. Half way down the cliff I slip, sliding down about six feet on my bottom. The tank at my side, scraping and dragging along.

"Dag gone-it!" I lay on my back, stunned, but afraid of tearing up James's scuba gear.

"Are you all right?" Jamie said, carefully stepping on down to me.

"Yeah. Guess I need to just slow down. This tank is not light."

"Here Lucas, let me help you," Darwin said, just below me he takes the tank and grunts it on down to the water. "Maybe we should have just rinsed it off back at home."

"Well... Yeah, but I wanted to hide everything inside of the back pack." Now we're all in the water, washing the scuba gear off. "Okay, that looks good. Let's get the stuff inside of the pack and get going."

Out of the water, Jamie reaches for the pack and we work to place the tank inside and then each of the items tucked in place, making the pack full. With some pushing and tugging, we get it zipped up.

"All set to go," Stevie said. We all lift and strain with each step, up the cliff side with the load.

"Amazing how light this is with all of us working together," Jamie said.

We are almost at the top, slipping in our wet shoes. Over to the wheelbarrow, we lift the back pack up and in it. Held steady, Darwin takes his turn at the wheelbarrow. We help balance the load as we roll on down the trail towards the park.

"We'll get this load back in its place. Tomorrow, I'll call everyone to see if you guys can come to the park to play," I quietly said, "No flashlights. Just like we came here to play in the park." The buddies all understood and started to reply, when in the distance, Tony came from behind the house on the left. "Remain true buddies, remain true," I said.

Tony had seen us, as he walks into the park, with his two buddies following behind.

We keep walking and pushing the wheelbarrow through the park. Tony may be about a year older than my brother and about medium build like my brother. From the short distance, Tony's evil smile comes across his face. His goons snicker to each other.

That look alone, made sweat come up on my forehead. He wears a torn black jacket, black greasy spiky hair, ripped black jeans and black boots. His two buddies are also dressed the same way. An awful feeling came across me. No one else was around to help us if needed some. Where is an adult when we really need one right now? His two buddies are also dressed the same way.

"So did you kiddies have fun in your little red wheelbarrow?" Tony asks sarcastically.

"Yes, it was all right," Jamie said, as we keep on walking and hoping he would just leave us alone. His goons laugh out and punch each other in a stupid gang way.

"Say! What's in the back pack?" Tony said, trying to stop our forward movement.

"Just some of our stuff," I said, walking at a steady pace. Jamie turns to see his reaction. The two goons mimics a walking dance, trying to be funny.

"Let me see!" Tony said, moving in from behind us.

Fear again has come and must be stopped. I turn to say, "No. This is our stuff." Tony now on us and reaches for the back pack.

Jamie pulls his arm back, and he then pushes her down. Angrily, I push Tony back as the wheelbarrow tips over, Darwin rushes in from the right.

Sirens blare from the road, as we all look up. OH, Thank goodness! It was Officer Clifford. He steps out of his police car. Blue emergency lights strobe on and off.

"Tony Watson! Come here!" Announces Officer Clifford from his loud speaker.

"Did you see these punks push me?" Tony yells and points at us. Stevie points back at him. We then set up-right the wheelbarrow and place the back pack back in it again.

Officer Clifford is directing Tony to come on over. We push on up to the road and pause to see what was going to happen. "You guys can go on," said Officer Clifford, and smiles at us.

We gave a short wave to our friend of the law. And so we push on, as Stevie and Jamie peek backs. Then Stevie said, "look," and we all watch Tony and Officer Clifford.

Out of hearing distance, Tony and his buddies is seen gesturing with their body and hands. Officer Clifford calms him quickly, and we faintly heard him say, "I saw the whole thing Tony and I will not tolerate any hoodlum antics from you!"

We push on even faster and laugh under our breaths. Jamie and Stevie giggle, then we all join in the humor. We're thankful that Officer Clifford came along.

We need to get far away, so we start to run. We try to hold the wheelbarrow steady as it wobbles with speed. I hope Tony doesn't get back at us.

We have had some clashes before. One of which Darwin had been hurt by one of Tony's friends. That is one nice thing I can say about my brother James. He may be mean to me, but helps to protect me and my friends. That is if James is around. Although when Tony is mean to me and James finds out, James will later confront him about it.

"Hey Lucas, you say you'll call us about meeting tomorrow? Stevie asks.

"Yeah" I reply, as we we're getting closer to our neighborhood.

"Why don't we just meet there again at a certain time?"

"I don't want this to seem like a set-up plan. If I call and ask if you guys can come play at the park, then it won't sound like I had it planned."

"Oh. I understand now."

"And no wheelbarrow or flashlights." Darwin said quietly.

"That's right Darwin." I whispered, "Remember, this is our secret. Not a word to anyone."

As we cross the street to Stevie's street, Stevie says, "Talk to you all tomorrow."

"Yeah, see you tomorrow." As he waves goodbye, Stevie runs down the sidewalk to his house.

The ranch style cookie-cutter houses are all painted in pastel colors. Darwin ramps the wheelbarrow up over the curb, as we are at Jamie's street. Jamie pats me on my back and said, "Later guys," as she turns, with her long hair swinging side to side. She stops, holds up the necklace and says, "Thanks again Lucas. You saved me." Darwin and I stand still watching our friend skip away. She has always been a good buddy.

As we walk along, Darwin whispers, "Is this going to work out like you think it will?" His hands in his front pockets and studies the sidewalk with each step.

I look over to Darwin and say, "I believe so. We find this discovery behind the park and we report it to Officer Clifford. We're doing the right thing."

Our walk with the wheelbarrow has slowed some to concentrate on our discussion. "Guess I'm afraid, even though we're doing the right thing, something is going to go wrong."

"All of the years I have known you, your always wondering and worrying about something."

"I'm just cautious about some things. That's all." Darwin kicks at a small rock on the sidewalk. We watch it bounce along, skipping on across the street.

"If you have those cautious feelings, that's okay," I said, leaning on his shoulder. In view is our house. My thought is now on cleaning up and putting away the scuba gear, before anyone comes home.

"I'll give you a call later pal!" I said, and push the wheelbarrow on across the street, as Darwin walks to his house.

"Sounds good! Mums the word." With a thumb up, Darwin turns and trots on up his driveway. All looks quiet at my house, just as I was hoping. I open the side door into the garage and push the wheelbarrow on in. Over to the corner where James keeps his scuba gear container. I unzip the back pack, to start the un-packing.

"What do you think your doing punk?" James shouts from the doorway.

Scared out of my wits, I scream and drop to the floor, while hanging onto the wheelbarrow. Why was he home so early? I thought, trying to keep the wheelbarrow from tipping over. "I... was just putting this... stuff away."

"What are you doing with Dad's wheelbarrow?" He yells and walks towards me.

His shouting annoys me, "We were just having fun with it." But afraid, I took a step back. James once got in trouble for hitting me, he won't do it again.

James looks down at the wheelbarrow, "Dad is going to be mad if you don't clean it up." This is a normal fight with James. He yells a lot when Mom or Dad is not around.

Probably makes him feel good, acting like a boss. Enough of the shouting already, "Quit yelling James! I'll clean it up!"

"And what do you have in the back pack, kid?" His shouting eases off, but still acting tough.

"It's my back pack!" I reach down to take it, when James moves quicker than a flying bat.

"Let's see what's in it!" Sternly he faces me down and opens the pack. The mask and snorkel plops out into the wheelbarrow.

James stare right in my eyes, "What did you do? You took my stuff again without asking!"

In a guarded stance, I reply, "I had to help find Jamie's necklace." He looks again and sees the silver scuba tank in there with the regulator. "You did what?" Before I could explain, he said, "You used my stuff without asking?" James was really mad.

"I ought to bust you." He grabs my shirt and pulls me in closer. I jerk back and he let go, then he grabs my arm.

"No James!" I said, trying to release his grip and lean back, "Let me explain." His right arm cocked back, ready to slug me.

"You're not even certified, you took my stuff, and went diving?" James was so angry, that slobbers flew out of his mouth.

I stretch my head back to avoid getting sprayed. No. Please don't hit me, I thought. "James! Please don't! Listen to me!" I plead. His arm drops and he pushes me back.

James relaxes a bit and steps back. Wipes his mouth on his arm, staring right through me. James shook his head in disbelief, as I straighten out my crumbled shirt. "I know it was wrong, but I had to help my friend Jamie"

"Why didn't you ask me to help get it?" Of course I already knew the answer to that one. "This is the dumbest, worst thing you have ever done."

CHAPTER EIGHT

Three Days of Hard Labor

"All right!" James's finger is in my face with his head cocked to the side, "Mom and Dad is going to love hearing about this one!" A devilish grin slowly appears.

"No. James please! I'll make it right. I promise!" This can not go any further than James and I, as this could blow the discovery wide open. My plea to him seem useless.

From a little brother's plea, James replies, "How are you going to make it right?"

"I'll do anything!" I motion with my hands out to the side and take a desperate deep breath.

James thinks, brushes his hair back and then replies, "*Okay. Anything?*" I agree by giving him a defeated nod. "This is what you will do!"

Afraid of what he is about to say, I reply, "James, just be fair about it. Okay?"

"Fair! Was it fair for you to use my stuff *again* without permission?"

"All right... What is it?" I said, nervously awaiting for the dreadful task. The last time I had to do something for him was awful.

One summer, a few years ago, James had a job working out on the old Davidson farm, cleaning out the hog house. I used his favorite fishing pole, when mine wasn't working right. By accident, I tangled up his line badly. And I couldn't untangle it, he had to cut all the line out.

So he had me shovel hog manure out for two hours. But to top it off, he shoved me into a nasty pile. And then he laughed at me. I wouldn't dare tell on him, because his pay backs are bad. Someday he will be sorry!

"This is what you will do. I have many yards that I mow for people. You will mow five yards for me, without being paid a single dime. It will take you about a day and a half to mow them."

"What? I don't know how you mow those yards!"

"No problem. I'll supervise you, and if anyone asks, you're in training!"

A day and a half isn't too bad. Oh! I better tell James about the crack in the valve. Better now than he finds out later. Because it could be bad if I'm dishonest and don't tell him. "Okay, I'll do it. But I need to tell you about your tank."

"What? Did you bust it too?" He said, as he grabs the pack and removes the tank to look it over.

"I accidently bumped it and now the valve has a crack in it." I reply, as fear races through my body.

"I don't believe this! You're going to really pay for this, Lucas!"

"I 'm sorry James. It was an accident! Yes, I will pay for it. Please don't tell."

"This could cost around $80 to $120 to get it fixed!" He slaps the tank, "You little snot!"

"I'll pay for it!" I pleaded. I guess I feel lucky James didn't hit me.

"You bet you will! You will now mow another yard and paint a chicken house for me!"

Shocked to hear of the large tasks ahead of me, I reply, "James! This isn't fair!"

"I'll be paid $100 for the paint job. That should be enough to pay for the damage!"

"How long will all of these jobs take me?" Now feeling frustrated with all of these jobs being placed on me.

"Let's see," he said, as he thinks and counts on his fingers, "About three - eight hour days, and we'll start work tomorrow!"

I gulp, with swirling thoughts of everything happening going through my mind and said, "I can't do that!"

"All right, then I'll let Mom and Dad know about this problem!" He replies.

"No! I'll do it! Maybe it'll go quicker if I have my friends help me." I said, as I look down in defeat. James acts like he just knew he had me over a barrel.

"Oh, No, you don't! You're doing all of this by yourself, with me supervising you. And no one else will be around. And no friends are visiting while we work! We're going to be busy."

"James! This is totally unfair!" I said, as I drop to one knee, feeling crushed by his demands.

"I am your supervisor! And you are my unpaid slave until these jobs are done!" His hand firmly on my shoulder and showing a heartless grin.

I have no choice. I can't jeopardize the discovery. This was suppose to have been so easy to follow the plans and present it to the law authorities. "I understand. It's not fair, but I'll do it."

"Next time, pal! Think before you act! In fact! Ask permission before you use someone's stuff!"

Yes, I knew that. But I felt it was important to Jamie, to get the necklace back. So she wouldn't get in trouble! "Okay James, you're right. I was wrong."

It was a simple plan, to borrow the scuba gear, dive down... Oh! Ok, exploring the cave got me. I did take a risk! Never the less, what I know now, and what I had found, I would do it all over again, and just pay the price!

"You better put this away for now and get cleaned up before Mom comes home. Tomorrow morning we'll start our first day of work., Slave Boy." James gruffly said.

I get up on my feet and feel lucky to be alive. I'm thinking about the discovery plans, what to do? I unpack the gear, wiping all the scuba equipment off with shop towels. I can't report anything for three days, I have to work.

James helps me place the equipment back in the containers. Then he said, "I'll take the take the tank to the scuba shop to get it repaired. Probably do that next week, when I have some free time".

I didn't say a thing. Better off if I didn't. As I'm thinking about my friends, who I can't see for three days. James and I leave the garage, to go in to get cleaned up. James stops and turn to me, to say, "Remember... If Mom or Dad asks what's going on, just say your in job training."

"I'll be teaching you how to mow yards and how to paint," he said.

"Yeah. Okay," I quietly said, as we went on in the house. Our Mother should be home soon and Father should be home around 6 o'clock from work. That's when we usually eat supper.

During my hot shower, the thought that The Buddies plans will be held up for at least three days, bothers me. I need to call my friends to inform them of my three days of hard labor. But I better wait until later to call them. When it's safe! What James had said earlier about "No Friends either", I don't want to set James off.

"Hello Guys!" Announces Mother from the kitchen door. The shopping bags could be heard plopping down on the kitchen table.

As I dry off and get out my clothes, I shout, "I'll be right out." I could hear James walk into the kitchen and the two of them start talking. Mother asks James about his fun day at Indiana beach. I listen closely while I comb my hair.

James said his day was cut short. Due to Danny, one of his friends, becoming sick. Could have been something he may have eaten.

Mother asks if anyone else became ill. He replies "No, we all had sandwiches, cheese fries, snow cones, candy apples, popcorn..."

"Oh! Well, no wonder he got sick!" She giggles while unpacking the bags. Finished from getting dressed and I walk on out to join them, now knowing why James came home early.

James replies, "What? Oh, No, He was fine until we went on the tilt-a-whirl, and then we rode on the bullet! Guess all of that fast spinning, and turning upside down, topped it off, but we all had fun."

We all laugh, then Mom asks, "So is he all right?" As she pauses between the sacks.

"We had to stop twice at a gas station on the way home, so he could go to the restroom."

I cover my mouth, as I remember the time when I ate some green apples from Grandpa's apple tree. Did I ever get an upset stomach. That was awful. I went into the living room to watch some television. James and Mother still talking in the kitchen. As I lay on the couch, I found on the explorer channel, geologists exploring a cave system. Oh yeah. That's me. Then I hear James say something about going out this evening with his friends, because he has some work coming up.

Mother knows James mows yards and paints some for extra money, so she doesn't ask any further questions. So with him gone tonight, I'll be able to call my buddies.

"Lucas! I'm fixing spaghetti and meatballs with garlic bread for supper. Did you do your chores?" Our Mother asks from the kitchen.

Oops, I forgot. I slowly slide off of the couch like a slug, and reply, "No, not yet." Now on my hands and knees, I get up to start on the dreadful chores.

"You have an hour before supper to get them done," she said.

"All right," I said, while walking to the trash can, which is under the kitchen sink.

"I forgot to ask you what you did today," She asks, clanging a pot free from the cabinet.

A warm scary feeling flushes through my body, afraid of what to say, "Uh... we played down at the cliffs, swimming, you know." I glance up towards James, who was folding up the empty sacks. He glances back for just a few seconds and then goes to take the sacks out to the garage.

"Don't you kids ever get tired of going down to the cliffs?" Mother asks, while putting away more groceries. "I'm not busy tomorrow, how about we go to the water park?"

Not ready for this sort of question. I gulp, "I can't." Not a good answer. Give her a good answer Lucas! "James and I were talking, he is going to show me how to mow yards tomorrow." Nervously, I drop some trash on the floor.

"Oh... That's nice of him to show you some responsibility. Maybe you can start making some extra money too."

James comes back in the kitchen. "James, that's nice of you to take Lucas with you tomorrow to show him how to mow." James cracks a smile and looks at Lucas.

"Yeah. Guess it's time he learns the ropes. He just can't be taking my yards though."

He replies, as he walks on through the kitchen to the bathroom.

"Oh no, Lucas can find his own yards. There's plenty of yards he can mow around town," Mother said, as I bag up and lift the trash out, and lug the trash on out to the garage.

I reply, "No problem." I had to get out of the kitchen, the heat is getting hot. "I'm going to trim the weeds around back," I shout from the garage. She says something about being careful. With the trimmers in my left hand, I open the back door with my right hand. A breath of fresh summer air is what I need.

Around the bushes, I hack away, releasing some frustration. Dandelions and rag weeds went flying. Then I heard a "PST." I look up and around, and then another, "PST, Lucas!" The trimmers drop right here by the bush. "Up here, stupid," James said from the bathroom window. Carefully I duck under a bush, and went up to the window.

"What's up?" I quietly said, looking up, beyond the bushes to the window screen. There is James's face up to the screen, then turns to look back at the door, as if he could be over heard.

Then turns back to say, "You said the right thing kid. Just don't talk about our deal." Before I could say a word, the window closes and he is gone.

Back down to pick up the trimmers, I crawl out of the bushes and look back. Yes, I covered myself well.

I said to myself, "It was your deal, not mine." With a deep breath, I need to finish this small chore. Like a broken record, the thought of my discovery, came creeping back in my head. The skeleton and the money bag mystery is waiting for me to come back.

Blades of grass and yellow blooms are clipped to death. Not even thinking what I was doing, my mind swirls thoughts of The Buddies plan. How we rediscover the cave, explore it again to find the skeleton and money bag there, just as we had left it.

And then report it as an emergency find to Officer Clifford. All of this makes my head feel bogged down, thinking about it. Before I knew it, I had finished my trimming chore.

Back in the house, I notice that Father was home. He was resting and reading the paper. We don't bother our Father much. He has a stressful job at the water department, and seems nervous a lot. I said to him, "Hi Dad," as I went to wash my hands. I heard him say 'Hello Son.' He doesn't have time to do anything with James and I, Mother usually does all of the parenting work.

Sometimes, Father will go out for a late evening walk down by the park and the cliffs.

He always goes by himself, 'to think', he says. We had tried to go with him, but he insists to go alone. His boots sit in the corner of the garage, muddy from his long walks. His muddy flashlight also is next to his boots.

He has said before, that he likes to walk down by the water. It can be quite muddy there. Later on after supper and during a quiet time watching television, the thought of calling my friends came to mind. James said he was leaving for a few hours with his friends. Soon after he left, I told Mom and Dad that I'm going to talk to my friends. So I go to my room, to call my friends.

Darwin is called first, and I explain the problem to my good buddy.

Darwin is worried, of course, and asks, "What are we going to do? What happens if someone else finds the cave?"

On my bed I lay, quietly discussing a new plan, I thought that I'll have no choice in the next three days. The phone cord twirling in my fingers, reminds me of our tangled mess.

If Mom or Dad is informed of me using the scuba gear, then they may relate scuba diving to the cave or I might be grounded for a week. I don't know. Also if I'm grounded for a week, then the plan would have to wait a full week before we can go on."

"Yes. That could be the worst problem to have. But what about the cave until you get back? And what do we do while you're working?" Darwin said, still struggling with a solid plan.

"The cave has been there for a long, long time. We have to feel safe that no one else will find it. Darwin, my best friend! We have to keep this our secret and stay calm. If you guys want to go to the park and just play naturally, kind of like your watching over the cave entrance, that's okay. Just don't act suspicious."

"But please, make sure the others don't act stupid. Like going over to look inside the cave or talking out loud about our secret. Someone might be watching you guys or even listening."

"Okay. We can take our baseball stuff and play some ball. Maybe stop to rest on the swings. If anyone asks where you're at, we'll just say you're doing a job with James."

"That sounds great Darwin. Just don't let anyone jeopardize our discovery. This is so

important to all of us."

"You're so smart Lucas. I understand and you can trust me to keep control of everyone. Even though I'm scared, I assure you everything will be fine."

"If it's too hard to keep control, maybe you can divert others from the area." I turn over to find another comfortable spot on m bed and to fluff my pillow.

"No, I'll be fine. I'll probably be so nervous and scared if I'm not there to watch over the area."

"All right. I'll call you tomorrow evening to see how your day went. I need to call the others to explain what we have decided to do. Okay? Later, Darwin."

"Sounds good. Later." Darwin hangs up. The clock reads 6:45 p.m. as I dial Jamie's phone. Again, I explain the problem to Jamie and what Darwin and I had talked about doing. Jamie has some questions and soon understands. She feels that James was too mean and harsh on me.

She said she would stay calm and help keep control. She also wants to come visit me while I 'm mowing.

I explain that visitors are not allowed, per my supervisor, James. She says he is a grouch! I laugh and agree with her. Stevie needs to be called next, as I say goodbye and promise to call Jamie as soon as I could after work.

Stevie answers the phone. "Hello Stevie. Are you somewhere so we can privately talk?" I quietly said.

"Huh... Mom is right here watching television with me." He replies.

"Can you go into the other room so we can secretly talk?"

"No... this is the only phone we have," He said, as he rustles the telephone, "We can just quietly talk here. She won't hear us."

"Ok Stevie, just say 'Yes or No' in our little talk here." I again explain the problem very carefully, so Stevie feels he is an important member of The Buddies. And that the Buddies are relying on him to be quite and calm.

When all of this is finally broken to Officer Clifford, and when the plan goes through as we had agreed upon, we might soon be hailed as heroes and with our picture in the newspapers. Stevie said, "Yes," and I had to remind him it's our secret. He again said, "Yes." I reminded him that it's very important and the death-pact wish hangs over all of us. Stevie said he understood by saying, "Yes."

"Okay, later, buddy!" I said, and hanged up, now feeling tired. I went back to the living room and told Mother, that I'm going to bed.

"Good night, sleep good," She said, giving me a hug and a kiss.

"Good night, Mother." Tomorrow is going to be a tough day. I have helped Dad mow our yard before, but not a whole yard by myself. Tomorrow, I have four or five yards to mow, with a tough supervisor watching over me. By tomorrow afternoon, I'll be dead tired, but I can do it. I know I can.

CHAPTER NINE

Work like a Dog

The smell of eggs and bacon cooking, awoke me out of a good sleep. While getting dressed, James pokes his head in, "Hope you got a good sleep boy! We're going to have a fun day!"

"Yeah," I reply, pulling a tee shirt over my head. Mother can be heard telling father to have a good day, as he heads out the door for work. Seems like that's all he ever does is work. No time for the family. Mother calls for us to come to breakfast.

In the kitchen, Mother has the table set and divides the eggs and bacon up between us. Then says, "So you're going to show Lucas how to mow yards today?" While buttering the toast.

"Yes. We have several yards to mow," James said, putting a fork full of egg in his mouth.

"What are you going to do with your money, Lucas?" Mother asks, and places toast on our plates.

James stops munching and we both look at her. Through the chewed bacon and toast he mumbles, "We have it worked out, Mom," as he continues to chew, and I look at him.

"Just be fair about it, James. I'm sure you'll teach Lucas everything about mowing yards the right way." Smiles and then tells me, "Lucas, I'm sure you'll do just fine."

"This will be different for me." Just helping Dad with our yard was all I knew.

With breakfast finished, James fills a cooler jug of ice water. "I'll be around here today doing house work. Stop by around noon and I'll fix us a sandwich.," Mother said.

"We'll see where we're at around that time. If we're not here then, don't wait on us," James replies. With that said, I sunk to the thought of having an awful day.

I look at James and then at Mother, looking for some kind of relief. "You boys have to eat, so don't work too hard," she said, patting me on my back. Out the door we head, with me carrying the cooler jug, ice water clunking and sloshing inside.

"Don't we need our mower and gas tank?" I ask James, who is walking like he's a macho man. Such a jerk he can be.

"Not the first yard we're going to do, Miss Mary has a mower and tank of gas for us."

Miss Mary lives a few blocks away, about a block to the south of where Stevie lives. She is a retired third grade teacher. I think James had her for the third grade at our School.

It's a nice warm morning and it's suppose to be near 90 degrees today. The news said that there is a chance of rain this afternoon. Hopefully James won't make me mow in the rain, but with him, I'll never know. A honk of a car horn from the main side street. It's Officer Clifford, he's making his rounds.

We wave, but James keeps walking. I would have stopped to talk to him, but again, James is in charge. Officer Clifford also waves and drives on. He is considered our friend, but if James is on a mission, there is not much socializing. Officer Clifford also knows James, like he knows all of the kids around town.

Out-of-the-blue, James says, "I still can't believe you took my scuba gear without asking!"

Surprised by his comment, I said, "Sorry." I can't believe he had to bring that up.

"Not even certified and diving by yourself. A very stupid thing to do!" He looks down at me.

"I said I'm sorry. It won't happen again." He grunts and marches on.

I have to walk fast to keep up to his pace and switch hands on the cooler jug to give my aching hand a rest. After another block, we reach Miss Mary's house. Soon I set down the cooler jug and scan the yard, James rings her doorbell.

The front yard is small, this may not take too long. Miss Mary answers and allows us to start mowing. James leads me around to a shed out back. Oh, No, the back yard is large. James opens the shed and pulls out an old push mower.

After showing me how to check the oil and the gas level. He explains how to prime the choke and set the start control to the start position. After two pulls, it starts, he throttles the lever up to the run position. "This old mower doesn't have a safety bar, which kills the mower if you let go," James explains.

Soon I feel comfortable with mowing. James explains where to mow, and what not to do, and then he is soon found taking a rest in the shade. Now feeling good, I pick up the pace a little more, "Slow down. Just walk normal and let the mower cut the grass," James shouts from the shade tree. I nod in agreement and pace myself. Before long, the first yard is finished.

After satisfying my thirst of ice water, James comes around to say, "Okay, now let's go to the next yard."

"That wasn't too bad," I said, as we put up the mower. James then went to talk to Miss Mary, and after a few words, she hands him some cash. We wave goodbye and walk on down the sidewalk.

Out of curiosity, I ask James, "For that size of a job, how much did you get paid?" I knew I wouldn't get paid anyway, I just wanted to know.

"That took you about an hour to mow, and I got paid $15," he said with a smile, "$20, If we had to use our own mower."

I didn't ask anymore about that, but figured that if we do four yards today at that amount, $60 would be made. Not bad. If James did that 5 days a week, he would make $300. That might explain how he has so much money. But I don't see him working that much. Maybe he charges people differently.

"Where is the next yard to mow?" I said, as we walk side by side, anxious to get these yards finished.

"Just around the corner is Mr. Thomas's house," James replies and points.

Another block and we 're there. "This yard is little bigger." James takes a drink from the cooler jug.

We walk into the yard as I look it over. The yard looks like it is twice the size as the last one we mowed. After getting out the mower, and with some instruction from James, I'm well on my way. This isn't a bad job after all! After some time and a few breaks, another yard is finished.

James said, "I'll collect this yard money later from him." We put the mower back in the shed and close the door. As we walk across the yard, James said, "You catch on quick! You did a nice job. Are you ready for lunch?"

Feeling more hot than hungry, I said, "Thanks. Yeah, I'm ready." Maybe by the time we get home, I'll be hungry. "Where are we going to go eat at?" The water jug half full, is a lot lighter than when we started. James takes it and douses himself with the ice cold water.

He hands it back to me and I douse my head to find relief from the heat. So refreshing! "We're about four blocks from home, so we'll eat there. We'll need to use our mower after we eat anyway."

"All right," I said, as we walk on towards home. Then coming up from behind us on bikes, are Tony Watson and two of his buddies. They look and say, "Hey."

We just look, while James nods and replies, "Hey." Tony and his friends didn't stop, They just nodded and went on, not to cause any problems. No problems here, as there must be some kind of mutual agreement between Tony and James.

I wanted to tell James about what happened yesterday, but didn't want to stir up any problems. Officer Clifford had it under control then and I felt that would probably be the end of it. James looks down and gives me a smirk. He didn't say a word, but it was as if to say, 'They won't bother us.' I hope there won't be any more problems.

Around the corner we walk, heading on down our street. My thought quickly goes to my Buddies, who are at the park, guarding the cave entrance. I just hope they stay calm and don't have any problems. I know that it shouldn't, but it worries me! The park is almost four blocks from here. I would love to go check on them, but know that's not possible until tonight.

Some distant laughter is coming behind us. We turn to see Tony Watson and his bunch riding by on the cross street, which is half a block behind us.

They we're heading towards town or to the park area. I hope they leave my Buddies alone. Now I'm concerned! James again glances at me. He must have seen something in my face. "If Tony or his buddies ever bother you, just let me know," He said. Shrugs his shoulders and says, "Him and I have an understanding. He won't bother you."

All I could say was, "Okay," in response. Even though there was a scene yesterday.

Now in view is our house as we keep walking, with me switching hands, carrying the water jug.

Once inside, Mother asks us if we're hungry. We reply that we were, as we go to wash up. "I'll get the lunch set out," she said, coming from the front room. "How are the mowing jobs coming along?"

James replies, "Good. Lucas is a quick learner." He dries his hands and gives me a smile, then tosses the towel on top of my head. I finish washing and pull the towel off of my head, I said, "Thanks, Bro." James can be nice when he wants to.

After a quick lunch, we head back out with a fresh cooler of ice water. James gets our mower out of the garage and checks the gas level in the tank. "We better top it off," He said.

"I'll get it," I said and went into the garage. Back to the mower, I fill up the tank. Soon we're on our way again, with James pushing the mower and me carrying the cooler jug. "Where are going next?" I said.

"Downtown to Mr. Saul's house," he said, pushing the mower along step by step. Mr. Saul's house. That's past the park, on the other side of town close to the reservoir bridge. All right! We'll be going right past the park. I can at least peek over to see The Buddies and see what they are doing.

"That's a good six blocks from here," I said. "Wait a minute." I sit down the jug and run back to the garage to get a piece of rope. I came back to tie the cooler jug onto the mower handle. "There! Now I won't have to lug the jug all the way there and back."

"Smart thinking! You can now push the mower."

"Still easier than hauling the cooler jug." I said and push on, with the jug swinging side to side. We all know this small town very well, or I thought we did, until we found the cave Hum, that's a good one.

We also all know almost everyone here in this community. And that goes to where they live too. "It will be a good walk for us and then we'll walk another six blocks over by the cemetery for the last job for the day. It's a big five acre mowing job!"

"What? Boy, am I ever going to be dead tired tonight!" I said. My body feels drained already from his information. James just laughs, and I reply, "Hey, I'm new at this. Remember?"

"You'll be okay." The heat of the day now upon us. A few large clouds overhead doesn't seem to help much. We turn the corner onto Main Street and then, two more blocks to the park.

My thought goes to the yards we will work today. I did three yards before lunch and two more to go, that means that the mowing work will be done today. But James said there will be three days of work I need to do. So tomorrow will be to paint the chicken house. How long could it take to paint a chicken house? Unless it's as big as a house!

There in the distance on the left, is the park. No one near the park entrance. Further on down the street, are three cars in the downtown area. A few people can be seen on the sidewalk. The trees to our immediate left blocks my view of the swings in the park and the cave area.

A faint sound of commotion of kids can be heard. I hope there is no problem! James and I march on, as every step gives me a better view of the park. Some cheering can now be heard from the park. There in the ball diamond are many boys, whom I know live in this area or go to the high school.

They're playing baseball, probably on evenly split teams. Looks like about eight on a team. James watches the game going on and slows up on his steps. I look beyond the game, past the out field, to the swings.

There sitting on the swings are Jamie and some girls from our class. Darwin is sitting on the ground in the grass next to the swings. A friend he knows in his class, also sits in the grass.

They are all watching the ball game going on. Stevie is not around. Maybe he went home for lunch. "Hey James," shouts a friend of James, from the dugout. "If your not too busy mowing, you think you can get away to play some ball?"

James stops and looks at me and then he shouts back, "I might be able to... I'll be back!"

"What about mowing?" I said to James, as we march on with James focused on the game.

"I'll get you started and then I'll come back to play ball. You know how to mow now, so there won't be a problem."

"I don't know... are you sure?" This is typical of James to do this. He gets a notion at any given moment to do something else, he'll go. Many times he doesn't finish what he starts.

Close to downtown, there on the southwest corner is an old Gulf gas station, that's where we get our gas. The southeast corner is the old town grocery store. Mom likes their meats there and I like the penny candy they have.

On the northeast corner is a Ben Franklin five and dime store. They have some neat things in there. On the northwest corner is the old Bank. We have our money in there, Dad says. He says they have been there for forty years.

Now that we're downtown, it seems to be busier than usual. A lot of the country folks like to come into this one stop-sign town. James and I rush on through, to cross the street.

Down just past the Bank is a Laundromat. Sometimes Mom takes our blankets there to wash them. As we push on, two more blocks to Mr. Saul's house. He is an old war veteran with a leg injury, so he needs help mowing his yard.

Across the street on the north side of town is an old Feed and Seed mill. Dad says, that many of the local farmers like to go there to have morning coffee and to plan their day's work. Houses sit next to these small businesses, when the town was moved up on higher ground. James and I look around at the sights as we walk on. Many of the people we know, so we wave and they honk back to us.

Soon we arrive at Mr. Saul's house and James gives me the directions on how he likes his yard to be mowed. Then he asks, "You know where the old cemetery is, over on Old Meshingomesia Trail?"

"Yeah," I said, but afraid of what James is about to instruct me to do. As I know he is going to leave me to go play ball.

"Next to the cemetery, is Mr. Clouses's lot. A fenced-in area that holds milking goats."

"Yes, I know about them." We like to look at them when we drive by the lot.

"You do this yard, which will take you about an hour, then head over there... it's about six blocks, just outside of town. In the back of the fenced-in area, is the milk house. On the north side is a small garage door, lift it and there is a riding mower, just like the one you used this morning.

Mow the whole five acre lot, with the deck up in high position, just to knock down the tall weeds and use our mower to mow along the outside of the fence, all around the fence.

Its real easy and the goats are friendly, they won't bother you."

"But James... this sounds like a lot for me," I said, wiping my forehead and then taking a swig of ice cold water.

"Lucas, you have proved to me that you know what you're doing. This will be easy for you! When you're done in a few hours, stop by the park to pick me up," James said, with authority and having confidence in me.

"How long will this all take me?" I said, trying to remember everything he told me.

"An hour here, and two hours over there. This will be it for your mowing part. Tomorrow we'll start the chicken house painting job." James has this all planned out and he does it well. He has done these jobs for several years, saving his money to buy things and to get ready to buy a car. He now has his drivers license and uses the family car when he can.

"By the time we get home, it may be 6 o'clock." I said, then took a drink from the jug.

"A nice full day of work!" He said and took a big drink, before starting to walk back to the park.

"Why do I have to mow the tall weeds, when the goats can just eat them?"

James is now walking backwards, trying to leave and says, "Goats don't eat everything like everyone thinks they do. There are several weeds they don't like to eat. Oh... Mr. Clouse said there is a full gas can next to the mower. See you later at the park, punk!" James turn and runs towards town, in a hurry to go play ball. I'd like to play too, but I must work to pay my debt.

With the heat boiling the asphalt into tar bubbles, I'd rather be at the cliffs, cooling off in the reservoir.

CHAPTER TEN

Wrestling Goats

It's almost 2 o'clock now, so I need to get busy. If all goes well, I could be back at the park in a few hours. Mr. Saul's yard is large with a two-story brick home nestled in the middle of it. The drive goes along the side of the home and under a side door canopy, then on back to the garage. I can see why it will take about an hour to mow. The yard is dotted with small trees and several flower beds.

James explained the cut pattern for this yard. A diagonal back and forth cutting is how Mr. Saul prefers it to be mowed. James said that not too many people cut their yard this way, but it looks nice cut this way.

Our mower starts with no problem and soon cuts its way across the yard. Around the trees and along the flower beds I push the mower. Careful not to nick the trees or run over anything except the grass. Up and down, back and forth, walking to the rhythm of the mower, all along the driveway and around the house. Out back around the garage and the back deck, and even more trees, trying to slow up my mowing.

The far back property sits on the edge of the reservoir. The final leg of my mowing takes me to the edge of the tree line. The beautiful view stops me in my tracks, as this is one angle I have never seen. How we love the reservoir!

A few more passes with the mower and then a final check of the trimming. Out of the corner of my eye, I notice a car driving up in the driveway. Not directing my attention to the car, I take a cold drink from the cooler. So refreshing! A man from the car walks towards me.

"Hello. You must be James's brother," said the elderly man. The small friendly man is walking with a limp and a cane. He reaches out to shank my hand, looking through thick bi-focal glasses.

I place the cooler jug in the grass, and shake his hand and say, "Yes. I'm Lucas Losure." My smile greets his smile and the warm welcome. He looks comfortable wearing a Hawaiian shirt, safari shorts and sandals.

"I'm David Saul. Glad to meet you. Are you helping James with his mowing job?" He said nicely and then looks across the yard.

"Yes, James is busy and has shown me how to mow yards." I reply, as Mr. Saul looks around the yard I just mowed. I feel like there could be a problem, so I said, "We have a deal worked out." The yard looks good to me. I hope he likes it.

"The yard looks good. You did a fine job and I'm sure James is fair to you. And you seem like an intelligent, hard working young man, so I feel you need something special."

Mr. Saul reaches back and pulls out his wallet. "Here is a tip for you," he said and hands me a five dollar bill.

"Oh... I don't know..." I reply, being caught off guard to his gift of thanks.

"Yes! It's all right! I appreciate good working young people and you deserve it!" He said with a warm smile.

"Well... Thanks, I appreciate the tip," I said, taking the bill in my left hand and shaking his hand with my right hand. I feel funny taking this tip, as James never said anything about this possibly happening.

"And you don't need to say anything about this to James either." Still, shaking my hand.

"Okay." Mr. Saul seems to understand what I am going through. Wow, this is great!

"Thank you Mr. Saul." I stuff the bill in my front pocket and smile with appreciation.

"No. Thank you and you can call me David." The heat beading up sweat on his bald head. "I need to get inside, so you don't work too hard and have a nice day, Lucas." As he walks to the back door, turns and waves goodbye. "It was nice to met you and I'll see you around town."

"Yes, thank you. Nice meeting you." I wave goodbye and pick up the cooler to strap it on the mower. That was nice of David doing that. The back door closes as I finish and push on. As I check out the finished yard work, proud of my work. Guess I can mow well after all. Down the drive I push on, to the next job. I wonder how many times James gets a tip from his customers.

He has never said, although James doesn't say much to me anyway, unless he is upset about something.

James said that the next yard is about six blocks away, on the east end of town. Main street leaves the north end of town and crosses the river, to meet the state highway. Across main street, I push on, past several streets on my way to the cemetery.

I may not know everyone around town or the county, but I do know the roads and landmarks. The cemetery and the goats in the fenced in area, are well-known landmarks.

Many of the houses on this end of town are older than most of the houses in town. After crossing another street and tipping the mower up onto the sidewalk, I pause to get a drink.

"Hello Lucas. What are you doing on this end of town?" A young girl asks, who quietly had rode her bike up from behind me.

Startled, I lower the cooler jug and turn to see Mary Fernades, a 4th grade girl from our school. "Hello Mary, I'm going to mow a yard over by the cemetery." Mary is a popular girl in her class and she is well liked. She must live over here somewhere.

"Oh. Making some money mowing, huh?" She straddles her bike, rocking back and forth.

"Yes. I'm helping my brother with his yards." I said, while strapping the jug back on the mower. "I have to get going, I'm on a time schedule. Sorry." With a wave goodbye, I push on.

"Goodbye. Drink plenty of water, it's a hot day." She said in a loud voice.

She must have heard that from an adult, I thought it was something my mother would say. Then just when I was well on my way, "Lucas. I think you're cute!" She shouts. Embarrassed, I keep going and just raised my arm to wave. Hope no one else heard that.

There probably are about three blocks to go, and I notice the properties are getting larger the closer I get to the edge of town. But now the sidewalks are going to end and I'll have to walk on the side of the road.

The tar and gravel road boils under the heat, as I aim for the large tar bubbles with the wheels of the mower. My old tennis shoes pick up sticky hot tar and some loose gravel with each step.

In the distance, I can see part of the cemetery which sits on a knoll. Because of the tall corn fields, I can't see the fenced-in goat yard, but I can see the tree tops in the same area.

If I remember right, the goat pasture, as many call it, is to the left of the cemetery. James and others call it a *goat yard*, because it has some nice trees on it and years ago there was an old farm house, and there were always goats around.

The rumbling of a vehicle grows louder as it comes closer behind me. Over my right shoulder I glance, as a truck horn beeps twice. As it rumbles by, a burly arm waves to me. Some loose gravel pings and bounces along after. The truck or person didn't look familiar, but I guess a lot of people know who I am. On down the road it rolls with a thin cloud of dust following it.

Closer to the corner, the old cemetery sits as peaceful as the last time I had seen it. To the left is the fenced in large yard. Among the trees are a few goats grazing in the shadows. The small wheels of the mower rumbling closer to the goat yard, causes a few of the goats to look up. The goats chew their cud as they focus on me pushing along. Between the munching, they bellow out a "Na-a-a-a". I couldn't help but to laugh to their calling. They look as cute as I once remember they were.

The yard has clumps of grasses and tall weeds like milk weed, thistle weed and other gnarly looking weeds which I don't know about. Some of the weeds look tough and may have to be worked with the mower. Tall maple and elm trees dot the yard to give shade to the goats.

The gate to get in is on the north side, back by the milk house. As I push on towards the gate, some of the ten goats follow me along the fence. They call out every minute or so, "Na-a-a-a." The gate lock was in place, but not shackled.

The owner knew the yard would be mowed today, so they left it unlocked. Several of the goats stand on the other side of the gate and call out, as if they were going to be fed. With the latch open, I slowly open the gate and squeeze through, quickly to close the gate. One goat stretches its neck around me, trying to get out. I lean into the goat and shout, "No," closing the gate before the goat could get its head through.

The goats are very friendly and one even nibbles at my shirt, as I turn to go pick up sticks in the yard. All of the goats are brown and white in color and seem to have full utters.

The goats are large, I suppose about 150 pounds each, as big as a Great Dane dog.

Under the trees are many limbs and sticks. The goats follow closely behind, as I pick up the limbs. Soon the goats know I don't have anything to eat and they go about grazing. The collection of limbs and sticks are piled up next to the gate.

Some of the goats are curious and rub the wood pile. They are funny to watch. After a while the whole four acres have been searched for down limbs and sticks. Now I can start to mow.

Quickly through the gate again, I close it behind me. A cold drink is needed right now. With a release of the strap, I gulp some cool water. Before I knew it, the gate knocks me to the ground! A goat pushes through the unlatched gate. The water cooler jug goes rolling and spills water. "No. Stop!" I said, getting up to upright the jug.

Another goat also follows, as I rush to close the gate. And another one runs behind that one, before I can close and latch the gate.

"Hey!" I shout as the three goats run to the corn field. "Oh no, not the corn!" Flat out full speed to the goats I run. They must be stopped and put back in the fence. The tender corn stock leaves are what they want.

The closest goat I grab around the neck and try to lead it back to the fence gate. Here I weigh 112 pounds and each goat out-weighs me, as I struggle and wrestle the goat back to the gate.

With a neck lock, I was able to unlatch and open the gate. Only to be met with more goats wanting to get out. I push the goat back in, blocking the other goats to quickly close and latch the gate.

The other two goats are munching away as if they were starved, as I rush over to grab another goat and wrestled it back to the gate. Again with one arm hanging on the struggling goat and the other hand unlatching the gate. This time the other goats just look and cry out, " Na-a-a-a-a." They knew something was going on. Back inside the gate she went with no problem.

And now for the last one, who wasn't there! What! Where did she go? Over to where she was at I run. No where insight. I call out for her, "Na-a-a-a-a," bellowing to get her to either come or answer back. The other goats bellow in response, "Na-a-a-a-a." Not who I wanted to call. Then inside the rows of corn, I hear, "Na-a-a-a-a" and some munching and rustling noises.

My ears follow the sounds inside a few yards to the goat, who is eating an ear of corn.

This is it, I need to get her back inside the fence. Never did I expect I would have to wrestle goats! Carefully, I force her around in the row, tripping on a corn stock. Down on my knees, I fall. On her neck I hang, to stay up right and then back on my feet to guide her out. To the gate we both wrestle. She didn't want to go back in. With persistence, I got her inside.

Oh Boy! Exhausted before I even start to mow, I plop myself down to rest. To catch my breath, and just above my head, through the fence - several goats are staring at me.

I couldn't help to laugh, with the sight of goats looking at me, up-side down. Soon rested, I stand up to get the mower ready. With the mower deck raised up as James told me to do, I start the mower.

The goats move away in fear of the mower. I wish I had thought of this before I had problems with them. Through the open gate, I quickly close and latch it behind me. I start on in, pushing around the fence perimeter, pausing some, to mulch up the tough weeds.

Many laps around the four acres in the summer heat, was quite a hot job. A short break in the shade of a tree with the water jug was a relief.

The goats must be use to me being around. They are over by milk house feeding on the grasses over there. Up again, mowing around the trees and make many more laps. No weeds able to withstand the power of the blades. A few hours pass, and now finish with the inside mowing. With the mower running, I exit the gate with no problems. To finish this job, I'll mow around the entire fence line.

With the mower turned off, I breathe a sigh of relief. The goat yard looks a lot better now, as the weeds are all cut down. Slowly I walk on down the road. One last time I bellow out, "Na-a-a-a-a-a," and the goats reply, "Na-a-a-a-a-a." The farm goats are fun to be around. They wore me out though, guess I'm lucky to have gotten them back in the fence without too much trouble.

The time to meet James in the park, must be getting close. It has been a nice hot day. Too bad I couldn't have spent it at the cliff with my buddies. The water feels so nice to me and swinging off the rope is so much fun. Again, my mind goes right to the cave in the park and the skeleton, whomever it is. It's not like the person died because they couldn't get out, something else must of happened.

Tired from a long day of mowing and wrestling goats, I push myself on down the road towards town. Half way to town, I stop long enough to get a drink. The ice is all melted, but the water is still cold. As I march on, the tar bubbles that were out earlier are not so common now.

Just up the road, I can see the sidewalks on the edge of town. It will be a relief to reach the town, as I'll be that much closer to home.

The sidewalks being uneven in places, proves to be a challenge pushing the mower. Some dogs in a yard, bark at me as I rumble the mower into town.

Now at main street, I turn left to head downtown. It seems like I've walked five miles today. Right now I feel like I'm dragging. My debt to James is harsh, but I understand and will pay it.

The quiet little town has a few shoppers taking their time getting a few things or just visiting. I wonder how the businesses can ever stay in business. It would be like me trying to run a lemonade stand on a cold day.

Up main street, pushing the mower with what energy I have left. The evening sun now above the western edge of the reservoir, the heat of the day has cooled some. Above the rumbling sound of the mower wheels, I can hear the faint sounds of a ball game going on in the distance.

The park is just ahead a few blocks to the right. A red car pulls onto main street from a side street and then turns into the park. I hope James is ready to go home, because if he isn't, I am going to go on.

Exhausted and hungry, I need to get home to rest. Five yards for my first day is pretty good I must say. The red car that pulled in earlier, now pulls out and leaves. Must have been a parent to pick someone up.

At the park entrance, I look for James among the players still playing baseball. There at shortstop, he is standing and talking ball trash to the other team. That's typical of him. Too tired to go on in the park, I push the mower into the grass next to the park drive and plop down in the grass to wait for him. I release the jug of water to quench my thirst.

Across the ball diamond, I see there is no one at the swings. Beyond the swings where the cave entrance is, no one is there. It would be a long time to hang around, so I don't expect them be there. We just hope to protect what we had found. As I scan over the park, by the left field fence, is Stevie's older sister, Tammy Thomas. She is alone, watching the game. Against the fence she leans, wearing cut-off blue jeans, a plaid short sleeve shirt and an old ball cap. Odd wear for a girl, but Stevie says she is different. Stevie said she likes to be alone.

Over by the first base dugout is Jamie, she is sitting in the grass area with Lori Lyman, who is in the 5th grade. No other Buddies are seen in the park. They must have went home for supper as it must be close to five o'clock. I don't dare try to alert Jamie, as James made it clear to me, no friends or visitors during work. I'll just call Jamie later tonight.

Jamie sees me and gives a quick wave. I give her a little wave back, to not seem too obvious. Over to where Stevie's sister was standing, Tammy is gone.

She is no where to be seen. James is walking towards me, so I get up and get ready to go. "How did you do?" James asks.

"Good. The jobs are finished," I said, moving slower now since I am rested and feel achy all over.

James releases the strap while walking next to me and takes a long drink. "Whew. You smell like a goat. You were supposed to mow the goat yard, not play with them."

"They gave me a little problem, but all is well and the yard is mowed."

"Problem, like what?" James stares at me, while we cross the street to head into our neighborhood.

"Three got out and I had to wrestle them back in." Tired from a day of work, I didn't feel like explaining what had happen. I must say, this is the hardest day of my life so far.

James laughs and laughs, trying to reply, but couldn't for laughing. Then he said, "I bet that was a sight." He starts laughing again and I didn't say a thing. On towards home I push even faster. All of my life, this is James, always bashing or having control over me. "You did latch the gate behind you, didn't you?"

"Yes James." This is about all I can say right now. A hot bath will feel good to me. James must have seen my face and heard something in my voice, he didn't say anything else all the way home. This is the first time that James has ever been speechless.

Inside the house, Mother was cooking supper. "How was your first day on the job?" She asks. The smell of hamburgers and French fries cooking, makes my stomach growl.

"*Hard*," I slowly said, and went into the bathroom to wash up. I'll eat first before I take a hot bath.

"James, is Lucas all right?" I hear Mother ask James. Then faintly I hear him say that I'm just tired from working hard. The hot soapy water feels great on my hands.

Supper tastes so good, even though I was dozing off while eating. And while in the hot bath, I was awaken to Mother knocking on the door, asking if I was all right. Ready for bed, I need to call The Buddies to see how their day went and if they had any problems.

In my bedroom, Jamie is first to be called. She is also getting ready for bed. Jamie said that everything went okay, some town kids came by first to play. And they swung on the swings and then they played kickball on the ball diamond. No one suspected a thing, even Stevie played like there was nothing going on.

They secretly kept an eye on the hidden cave entrance. While they played kickball, there was some little kids with their parents, who played over on the swings and monkey bars. She said It was amazing that they knew the cave was right over there, but no one else did.

I told her The Buddies did a wonderful job in keeping the secret to themselves. She asks how my work went today. I explain that it was hard, but getting easier. I'll be glad when it's over.

As I was ready to fall asleep, I must call the others as I had promised. Jamie and I said goodnight. Darwin is watching television and he said basically what Jamie had said.

All went well and there were no problems. Later on, an argument did happen in the all-teenager baseball game.

Tony Watson argued an out call against another teen boy and several teens had to break it up. Darwin said they just laughed as they watched from the swings. Stevie was a little hyper, but they settled him down by playing a little game themselves. He said The Buddies misses me and will be glad when we can get back together. I said I will be glad too. I'll call again tomorrow.

Stevie is happy to hear from me. He said he was my good Buddy and that the day went fine. There was other kids who came to play and no one knew of anything and The

Buddies acted like nothing was going on. I told Stevie to keep up the good work and I'll call him again tomorrow. I must have been tired, I don't remember telling Stevie goodnight.

Darwin is watching television and he said basically what Jamie had said. All went well and there were no problems. Later on, an argument did happen in the all-teenage baseball game.

Tony Watson argued an out call against another teen boy and several teens had to break it up. Darwin said they just laughed as they watched from the swings. Stevie was a little hyper, but they settled him down by playing a little game themselves. He said The Buddies misses me and will be glad when we can get back together. I said I will be glad too. I'll call again tomorrow.

CHAPTER ELEVEN

The Chicken House

In my sleep, I could faintly hear James say, "Wake up Lucas. It's time for breakfast. We have a busy day ahead of us." I just knew it was a nightmare, as I haven't been a sleep long.

Nightmares can be so real. James is shaking me to get up, as I said, "No." Through my sleepy eyes, I can see James standing over me. "What?" I ask and glance over to my clock. The red display reads *08:20*.

"You can't sleep in, we have work to do. Get up!" James says, flips back my covers and turns to walk out. I moan and slowly get up, oddly I still feel stiff and sore all over. The last time I have felt like this before, was when we had a rough football practice. After getting dressed, I go to the kitchen for some breakfast.

James is in the living room watching a fishing show. With a glass of milk and a Danish roll that mom had made yesterday, I ask James, "Where is mom?" She is no where around.

"She left a little while ago to go visit Grandma," He said, with a bite of a roll and a glass of orange juice in his hand. "She made us sandwiches to take on the job as I told her we'll probably be busy all day."

With my mouth full, I groan. All day long painting with James supervising me. What a joy. If I can just listen to his instructions and keep quiet, I'll be all right. He said three days of labor and this is day two. Maybe if I work hard and faster, today will be the last day. As I was just about finished with breakfast, James came into the kitchen and said, "Get your back pack when you're finished."

"Why?" I ask, as I place my plate in the sink.

"You'll need to haul our lunch to the next job."

"How far do we have to walk today?"

"We don't walk today, we'll ride our bikes," he said, while getting out a plastic container with a lid. James takes some sandwiches out of the refrigerator and puts them in the container. I wanted to ask where and what we're doing today, but afraid of getting a nasty response. He also gets out another container and turns to say, "Well, what are you waiting for? Go get your back pack." Out to the garage, I got the back pack and came back to the kitchen. James loads the pack with containers of sandwiches, potato chips and cookies.

With the cooler jug of ice water, the back pack was almost full. James then goes to the bathroom and comes back with two old towels and a roll of toilet paper. "What's these for?" I ask, pointing at the towels and toilet paper.

"It's going to be a hot day, so we can wipe off sweat with the towels and the toilet paper, if we have to do number two," he said with a devilish smile.

"So there isn't a restroom to use while we're there?"

"No. Everyone will be gone and the house will be locked. So if we have to go to the bathroom, we just go out in the corn field, dig a little hole with our shoe and go. Then just cover up the mess."

I try to imagine doing this and reply, "You're kidding?"

"No stupid. This is normal out in the farm fields. Let's get going." Out the back door James went, as I follow him, lugging the back pack.

"Where are we going and what kind of work will we be doing?" I just had to ask.

"The next two days *you'll* be painting a chicken house out at the Davidson old farm."

My mind still trying to visualize using the restroom out among the corn stocks. On my back I secure the back pack, as James jump on his bike and pedal down our driveway. With me on pursuit to catch up to him, the back pack shifting back and forth on my back. The rhythm of the ice water clanging and swishing inside the pack.

Before long, we were leaving the south end of town on a paved country road. It's another hot summer day, with only a few clouds in sight. I'm not exactly sure where the Davidson farm is, but I think it's a few miles out here. I'll just follow along and tolerate being with James. Maybe someday James will regret how he had treated his only brother.

We took the next road to the left and the only sounds heard are the bike chains rattling around the gears.

James's ten-speed mountain bike is faster than my three-speed banana bike, so I have to pedal faster to keep up. Another mile we ride on, corn fields after soybean fields and so on. Farm houses are few in many blocks, hidden among large trees which are outlined with barns, silos and grain bins.

James takes a turn down a grassy lane and so I follow. Along a fence row on the tractor path we push on and to the left is a large farm with white buildings. In the near distance is a long and low building in a lot surrounded by chicken fencing. All around the farm are corn fields.

Up to a chicken lot we pedal. The chickens in the lot scatter to our bikes dropping against the fence. "This is it," James said, holding his arms out to his sides. I slowly release the back pack and lower it to the grass, as I study the long chicken house.

It looks to be twenty feet long and eight feet wide with a single sloping roof from one side to the other side. This doesn't look too hard, I can probably paint it in one day.

"Over there by the gate are cans of paint and the other stuff we need," James said. We walk around the fence corner, as a German Sheppard dog scares me, barking from around a pine tree.

James laughs and says, "Old Laddie won't bother you. He just barks at strangers until he gets use to you." I just watch him, as he stays under the tree and keeps barking at us.

At the gate, James says, "Keep the gate closed and locked at all times, or the chickens may get out." The gate latch is very simple, lift up the latch, open the gate, close the gate and drop the latch.

The chickens are mostly white chickens, scratching and pecking at the ground.

They have the grass all worn down to the dirt. Looks like about forty chickens running around, most of them have red heads and red wallers under their beaks. "The chickens won't bother you, so just ignore them."

We pick up the paint and supplies and quickly go in the pin. The chickens move out of our way as we set down the paint supplies next to the chicken house. "I should be able to paint this in one day," I said, looking over the small building.

James replies, "Yeah, but you have to scrape it first." My smile must have turned up-side down. James punches my shoulder and says, "You knew that, silly boy."

"Oh, Yeah I knew that." Darn it, I didn't really know that. It's just an old chicken house. Why should it have to be scraped? I can't ask James that question. Instead of finishing today, it looks like I'll be here tomorrow too.

James explains anyway, that any loose paint has to be removed first by scrapping it. Back and forth, up and down, to chip off loose layers. He said the best way is to start at a corner and scrape from the top to the bottom. And work my way all the way around.

James shows me, as loose paint chips go flying. Then he went back over it in a different direction and some more came right off.

"See how easy it is, now you do it," he said, while handing me the hand scrapper. This doesn't look too hard. I went right at it and no paint chips came off, so I moved on up the wall. "You'll have to push harder," James said.

Oh, this could be tough after all. After some muscle, I was able to get it to flake off. "There you go, now just keep it up and I'll be right back." He said.

I shouldn't be surprised, but I had to ask, "Where are you going?"

James walks away, turns and says, "You're doing a fine job. I'm taking a break."

"Thanks." James is now out of the gate and go towards the farm house. He is certainly playing a supervisor's part. My job is to work for him to pay my debt. The summer heat again heats up. Chickens peck and scratch the ground, seem uninterested in what I was doing, although some were pecking at the paint chips which litter the ground. "Don't eat those, you might get lead poisoning." I giggle to myself, as they don't seem to care.

The morning time seems to move quick with one side scrapped. Lucky me, the next side is in the shade. My arm feels tired from the scrapping work, so I'll try my left hand. Awkward as it seems, I soon got use to the repetitive action. Around the windows was a little tricky, but it all went well.

The sun looks to be about high noon as I take a rest against the tattered wall. I wonder what happen to James, he has been gone a few hours. Suppose now is as good of a time to have lunch.

Out of my back pack, the ice cold water tastes great. Mom made one of my favorite sandwiches, ham, pickle and cheese with catsup and mustard. Yummy! Although the chickens became curious to what I was eating and came close to try a peck of my sandwich. But I just shoo them away.

I made a mistake by giving a few pinches of bread, others came squawking to get some too. Before I could get up on my feet, a few had pecked from my sandwich.

My shouting didn't faze them. They act like they were starved to death or they never tasted anything so delicious in their life! The white feathers flew with the flogging I was getting. I don't know how, but I was able to grab the back pack, cooler and what's left of my sandwich, and get out of the pen. A few feathers follow me out. "What was that all about?"

Down in the grass I plop, next to the gate to finish my lunch. The chickens pace just on the other side, some poking their heads through the chicken wire, begging for more of my sandwich. "No. This is mine." I look to take a bite and see where peck marks was left. "I don't suppose you guys have any slobbers."

As I enjoy my lunch, I could hear a low growling noise over my right shoulder. Slowly I look to see the German Shepherd dog sitting just a few feet from me.

Carefully and slowly I take another bite. The dog stares at my sandwich. "Don't they feed you either?" James said his name was Laddie. "Okay Laddie." I pinch off a piece. "Here you go." I toss it to him and he grabs it in air, and munches it down. "Pretty good isn't it?" The last bite is mine, as I look in the pack to see what else we have.

Potato chips and cookies. The other sandwich is James's. Laddie and I had our share of the lunch. "Taking a lunch break, Huh?" James said from afar. Laddie and I look towards James. Laddie barks and runs to greet him.

"Yeah. It's time and I didn't know when you would be back." James looks like he just came from swimming somewhere. His hair still wet and roughed up.

His wet towel is draped around his neck. "What have you been doing?"

James gets out his lunch, replies, "Just took a swim in the pool."

"A swim? Where?" I couldn't believe what I had heard. Here I am slaving away in the hot sun, while he is swimming somewhere nearby.

"Over by the farm house. They have a pool, but don't you worry, you have work to do." James takes a drink from the jug and then tosses a piece of bread through the fence to the chickens. How likely this is of James, knowing I was cooking in the heat and he's cooling off in a pool. "Just remember, I am your supervisor."

"Yeah." I wanted to say more, but instead, pick myself up to get back to work. I gave him a dirty look and he gave me a laughing smirk. In the shadow of the roof, I scrape and scrape. Soon to go around another corner.

Now I'm in the sun again. Between the strokes of the scrapper and wiping away sweat, I swat at an annoying deer fly. Sometimes not knowing it's there until I feel a painful bite. The chickens try to get the flies at the lower level, but up higher I have to deal with them.

Another drink was needed and a minute in the shade, I look to see James was gone again. Across the yard I look towards the fields and the house. No James. From here I couldn't see a pool. There are many trees between here and there. Under a shade tree, Laddie lays resting. I bet James is in a nice clean pool. There is nothing I can do about it and I don't dare go over there to get a refreshing dip, unless James allows me to.

After cooling off some with some water and my towel, it's back to the scraping. Paint chips flies up in my hair, many sticking to my sweaty skin and causing me to itch.

Oh, I would love to be down at the cliffs with my friends right now. My mind drifts to how they're doing at the park. Are they watching over the cave? Or has it been rediscovered? Or has anyone blown the secret? No. I have to think positive. Jamie and Darwin, I trust has it all under control.

With the chickens, scraping paint, swatting flies, wiping away sweat, flying paint chips and taking a drink break, seems like hours have passed by. I can hear James talking to Laddie and laughing. On my last wall, James comes through the gate, shooing back the chickens. "Looks all right Lucas," he says while coming alongside of me.

"Doesn't look too bad," I said, still scraping and not missing a beat. I was hoping he would say that it's time to head home.

"Are you sure you're scraping hard enough? Looks like some can still be scraped off."

James has another scrapper and pushes hard, gouging the wood. I just glance and keep scraping, not saying a word. "Looks good," he said and goes right on scraping. Around the corner he goes and I hear him say, "All right. Tomorrow you can start painting." I gave a sign of relief. "It's probably close to five o'clock. Let's call it a day." That's the best thing I've heard him say all day.

"I'm ready." We pick up the supplies and place it back outside of the gate. I wanted to go dive in the pool, but James never offered, so I'll just forget it. I was exhausted anyway. But it would feel real good to cool off in a pool with this heat.

With a last swallow of cool water, I pack the jug in the pack and sling it on my back. We pedal down the grassy lane to ride on towards home.

James had a nice day at the pool, while I worked hard. So that is why he is pedaling ahead and I am dragging behind. We will soon be home, to relax and get cleaned up. My mind drifts away to how my friends did today and what may have happen. This evening I'll call them. The Buddies secret about the cave, the skeleton and the money bag, gives me a sick feeling in my stomach.

Even though we have it all secretly planned out, the idea of all this going through without any problems scares me. And then it would be tough to explain why we hid our findings and didn't report it to the authorities. This is risky, but I feel like we have a good reason to do it this way.

Back into town, I must have caught my second wind as I'm almost even with James. Even the back pack tries to slow me down. Just up ahead, there is some girl riding her bike. Hey, it's Jamie. She is riding on the other side of the street, coming towards us. She stops as she sees us coming, she just looks as she also knows how James is.

And cautiously she waves at me and I wave back. As we ride on past, I cup the side of my mouth with my right hand and say, "I'll call you later." James peeks back over his left shoulder to me as we keep on riding. Not saying a word, I know he didn't want my friends around while we're working.

But now, we're not working, we're riding home. And just now in sight is our house. Mothers' car is in the driveway. Dad usually comes home later.

After getting cleaned up and some pizza for supper, I start to feel sleepy while watching some television.

Better call my friends, before I fall asleep. In my bedroom, laying on my bed, I call The Buddies on the telephone to see how they did today. The Buddies said there wasn't any problems. They kept quiet and had checked on the area off and on all day. Some teenagers came to the cliffs to swim and they soon left. Other kids came and went from the park.

No suspicious persons were around. The Buddies acted like nothing was up. One more full day of work, my friends. I said good night to my Buddies. And that's all I remember.

Again I am awaken, this time by Mother, saying, "Lucas. Lucas, it's time to wake up. James wants to get an early start today. And breakfast is ready."

Slowly I crawl out of bed, trying to wake up. "James said you're doing a fine job." My arms and back ache again today as I flex them, while grimacing.

"Yeah. It's going along okay," I said, not surprised that James would say something nice to our Mother and not say it to me.

Too tired to get dressed, I ate and finish breakfast in my pajamas. Soon to get dressed and packed for the last day. Mother says, "It's cloudy outside and there's a chance of rain today."

James from the other room replies, "We can't paint in the rain, we may have to wait until tomorrow."

With hearing that, I sternly said, "No. It will be a nice day." I froze in my tracks, as I should have not said it like that. It could sound suspicious.

Mother walks behind me and put her arm around my shoulders, asking, "Lucas. Are you all right." I could hear James walk into the kitchen.

"Yeah." The need to think fast came to me. "I'm just tired and want to finish the job today."

"Paint won't brush on wet wood, silly," James said, standing across the room.

Mother snaps her finger at James and said, "Maybe it won't rain and will be a nice day."

"That sounds good, lets go James," I said, trying to be positive.

"See you boys this evening," Mother said, as we walk out to get on our bikes. We turn and tell Mother goodbye, then James and I pedal on out of the driveway.

"Listen punk. I am the supervisor and you're my grunt. If we ride out there and can't paint, you will work for me another full day," James said angrily, riding close by me.

"Okay. Sorry James, I'm tired and just want to get my debt paid off." That's about all I can say and it hurts me to tell him I'm sorry. But I have to be careful not to sound too pushy and like I have something planned for tomorrow.

"Tired of working? Welcome to the labor force. Yeah, you're only 12 years old now, but someday you'll understand. That if you ever want something and Mom or Dad won't buy it for you, you'll have to buy it yourself. And you'll need a good job to get that money."

We ride on out in the country, not saying another word. Sprinkles of rain fall on us and it feels good, but not a good sign.

But as soon it started, it stops. I was thinking about what James had said about wet wood and he is right.

Someday I will understand about the work force, but right now I just want to grow up and have fun with my friends. At the Davidson farm, the grass is wet and the sun is trying to come out. The chickens are out working the ground again. They must do that every day. The chicken house didn't look wet, but James looks it over and even wipes his hands across it. "I don't know about this," he says.

I look at it and then up at the sky. "Looks good to me. Let's give it a good try."

He looks up and around, and says, "We'll see." He goes over to the supplies left by the Davidsons and gets the paint tray ready. I go over to help and he hands me a paint roller. After mixing the paint and pouring it in the tray, the stupid chickens come around, thinking we're going to feed them. James shoos them away.

"Let's see how it does." He rolls the roller in the tray and starts at a corner. The white thick paint goes right on and then James puts the roller back down in the tray. Looks close at the layer of paint on the wood and says, "Well... all right, go ahead and paint just like I did."

Up the wall with the roller with fresh paint. It rolls on good, covering the corner and so I move onto my right. I look at James and smile, then say, "Looks good. Covers real good." The roller on a short pole makes work easy, as I keep moving on.

Then after a while, I notice James wasn't around. He must have taken off again.

Better off that he is not around to pester me. There is Laddie walking around the barn.

This rolling paint job is easy and fun, I now feel good with this job. From the other side of the chicken house, comes a chicken squawking noise. A few chickens must be having a fight, as I turn to look around the corner. To my surprise, is a red fox getting after the chickens.

I shout and wave the paint roller at the fox. But the fox keeps chasing the chickens and I yell even louder and even jab at the fox with the roller. A chicken breaks free and the fox growls at me. I shout and jab, when from my right, Laddie hurdles the fence.

Laddie surprises the fox and pounces onto it growling and snapping The fox slips through the fence and Laddie clears the fence again, giving chase across the barn yard.

Around the chicken pen, there are feathers everywhere. The poor chicken who was jumped, had many feathers pulled from its back. It must be traumatized from the attack and just stands there, and then shakes more feathers free. The poor thing.

Soon it goes right on scratching the ground with the others, just like nothing ever happen. Again I look across the barn yard and no canines are in sight. The chicken didn't have a scratch on it, but looks funny with half of its feathers gone. Good thing its summer time, it won't need the feathers for a while.

All that's left is the trim painting, but it must be past lunch time. The day looks half way decent. The clouds still hang over, but not a drop of rain.

After lunch, I got ready to trim out the chicken house, when James comes back.

"How's the painting going?" He said. Again he looks refreshed and like he just woke up from a nap.

"All right." I said, while I stir the paint, making sure it was ready. James walks on around the house, looking it up and down. He studies the job as if his life depends on it.

"Looks good, Lucas," he said with a smile. Wow, a real compliment. That's unusual.

I look at him with a smile and said, "Thanks."

"You did a good job so far, Lucas. Do you know how to trim it out now?"

"I believe so. With a small dip of the brush, you go around the window frame careful not to get any paint on the glass. Around the door frames, brushing the paint on all edges."

"Guess you don't need me to watch over you." James smiles and gets out his lunch. "I'll be back in an hour." He walks across the barn yard towards the house, with his lunch. The pool must be wonderful. James has it easy now, until I pay off my debt, then he will be doing his own jobs.

It wasn't long before I was finished. My debt is paid in full and I'm ready to go home. James then came back and looks over the chicken house. And says, "Okay, it'll do." We pack up and ride on home. Since it was only four o'clock, I got cleaned up and decide to go to the park. Our Mother wasn't home and James is taking a nap.

There on the park swings was Jamie, lightly swinging back and forth. She is so glad to see me, she gives me a hug. That must be what I needed as I now feel good. She said Stevie and Darwin just left for home. She said it was another good day. Over through the trees and brush I could barely see the dark entrance.

Excitement grew inside as the plan will soon come together. We both swing together on the swings and quietly talk about our plan. The time has come for us to go home, tomorrow will be the big day. With her hand in my hand, we leave the park together. The body aches I had earlier today, are now gone.

CHAPTER TWELVE

Back to our Plan

The Buddies all know of the plan and I can't wait. This is going to be so cool! This has been played over and over many times in my brain. It will work, and I couldn't see any problems that would stop us now. "Lucas, I want you to go shopping with me today," Mother said.

About to cough up my cereal, I look up to Mother, to quickly say, "Mother please, not today. I'm tired from working and I want to go have fun with my friends." Disgusted that she has a plan for me *today*. James is laughing in the living room.

"But there is a big sale going on and we need to get you some nice school clothes."

Oh no, not today. No. "Can't we please go tomorrow?" The Buddies plan must happen today.

"Oh... I suppose, but tomorrow is the last day of the sale, and you really need something nice for school."

"Thanks Mom, we'll go tomorrow." That was a close call.

I better hurry up and get out of here before something else comes up. Out the door with my good baseball hat and a towel, I hurry along. The feeling inside of me is great. The sun is out and its going to be a wonderful day. The Buddies are probably waiting for me.

The plan will just be a normal day at the park and cliff. Then the scene will take place at finding the cave entrance. At the end of the street I pause, and look around to see if any of the others are coming. No Buddies are seen, just a few men walking down the sidewalk and in the other direction, some ladies are talking out in a front yard.

On towards the park, way down the road near downtown, a tractor is moving. It might be too early as I believe the time is almost nine o'clock, but if The Buddies are as excited as I am, they're probably at the park already.

At the park, there is no one around. Maybe they're at the cliff idling some time. Over through the small trees and brush I look, and a chill runs down my spine. While walking, I turn to look behind me, as it feels like someone is watching me. Just a funny feeling I have.

Up the hillside to the cliff I hurry along. Birds and squirrels are active this morning, singing and playing in the trees. A gentle breeze blows from the reservoir. It seems like I have been away from here for a week. What a sight! Small waves break up the sun shimmering on the waters below. Along the shoreline are a few fishing boats working the edges for bass. How wonderful it is to be back here again.

It's easy for me to see The Buddies swinging off of the tree rope, laughing and having fun. Behind me from afar, is the sound of someone talking. Across the cliff and down towards the park, I walk to see who might be coming. In the distance by the park entrance, are The Buddies.

"Hey." I shout and wave from the middle of the hillside trail. They saw me and yell back, now running like they're in a 100-yard mad dash. I laugh as the three of them seem to be racing for the finish line. Darwin seems to be out in first place, with Jamie right behind him and then Stevie running for his life. With 50 yards to go, Jamie is now even with Darwin and Stevie laughing between huffs and puffs.

With their towels flapping behind them, they start going up the hillside trail. Jamie now takes the lead with Darwin straining to get ahead. Stevie slows some and says, "You guys cheat."

Jamie now a yard ahead, says, "Yes," and gives me a high five as she flies by. Darwin then races to me, saying, "Oh man!" Stevie runs right up me and gives me a pat on my arm, wiping his towel across his face.

Jamie comes back smiling as I say, "Nice race." Jamie is wearing flip flops, and replies, "And you are wearing Flips." She laughs, flips her hair back and points a foot out.

Darwin replies, "Hey, I 'm wearing sandals." We all laugh and slowly walk on up the trail.

Stevie said, "You guys cheated because it wasn't a fair start." We laugh again and Stevie keeps saying, "Cheaters." We then go to the cliff to sit and to talk a little about what's been going on and how bad my jobs were. But soon we were quietly talking beneath the oak tree about the plan. Excitement grows again. Stevie asks some wild questions, but The Buddies came together to focus on how it all will work out.

My ideas on the plan came from what we learned in school and had seen on television.

The 'accidental' finding of the cave entrance, the skeleton and the money bag.

Officer Clifford will question each of us and we will have the same story. There may be other authorities who will also question us. Stevie asks about what James knows. I explain that the scuba gear was only used to find Jamie's necklace and nothing else. No one will know about the underwater entrance, just The Buddies.

With a twig, Stevie draws in the dirt and Jamie twirls a dead leaf, while no one says another word. Darwin watches them and is probably trying to visualize how our plan will work. With the need to go on with our plan, I said, "Do you guys have any questions? We need to get going."

Darwin looks up and says, "No, I believe we're ready. We all *just* have to remember *only* the finding today." Jamie and Stevie look up to listen.

Darwin understands it. And so I reply, "That's right. Not what we had found before or had planned. Just remember the death-pact wish."

Stevie has a puzzled look and says, "But if we tell Officer Clifford, won't it break the pact?"

"No. Remember, the wish is only for us to not tell anyone, until the time is right. And after the finding, the time will be right. Officer Clifford is our friend, so we'll go get him first." To make sure we're not over heard, I look over my shoulder. "Let's go to the park and play, then I'll make the discovery."

"Lucas, why do you get to make the discovery?" Stevie asks.

"He's the one who found the underwater entrance, silly," Jamie replies, with a flip of her hand, as he already knew how it was discovered.

"I also went to great pains to make this happen. Like climbing inside the cave, dodging the bats and almost got stranded inside of the cave."

"And then Lucas had to pay a debt to his brother for using his scuba gear," Darwin said.

Stevie winces and says, "Yeah, you're right. Okay. I'm ready, let's go." Excitement gets Stevie up on his feet first and then the rest of us get up. Stevie takes off running.

"Stevie, let's just walk." I said, as together we all walk the trail down to the park.

"Sorry, it seems like Christmas morning," He said excitingly.

In the park, we turn right to go along the out field fence, towards the swings. No one is seen around the park and no one is up by the road. Over by the swings, Jamie says, "Let's swing a little, before we go into town."

The rest of us look at Jamie and Stevie says, "Huh." A big smile was on her face and I got it.

"Yeah, that sounds good." I said, nudging Darwin and smiling. Darwin winks and smiles back.

"But, I tho..." Stevie replies, as I stop him short with my hand. My eye catches his eye and I nod with a smile. "Oh...

That sounds good." He said, finally catching the drift. This wasn't a part of the plan, but Jamie plays it up real good. This was a good play by Jamie, in case someone might be listening. The Buddies swing and hang around. Then I glare and go over to the trees to start the find.

"Where are you going, Lucas?" Darwin asks.

"I think I see something," I reply, looking intently past the small trees. The others soon follow me, as I walk through the trees to the brush.

"You see a rabbit?" Stevie asks and then snickers.

"Oh wow! Look at this, it's an opening. Like a cave!" Closer to the opening, I pull back some vines to get a closer look. The others are right behind me.

"Oh my gosh! It is," Jamie said, acting to peer over my shoulder. Darwin to my

left, and steadies his hands on my shoulder.

"Hey. This is neat!" Darwin says, while Stevie worms his way between us.

"Let me see!" Stevie then says, "Ooh... it's dark in there."

"This is great, you guys!" I said, as this is just as exciting as if we really did just now find it. The plan goes on and I said, "I'll go home to get a flashlight, so we can explore it."

"Do you think we should go tell Officer Clifford first?" Jamie stops me in my steps to leave.

"No, I want to first see inside before we report this wonderful find. You guys wait right here on the swings and I'll be back in a few minutes. Don't hang a round here, as someone might see you and ruin the discovery." I run a few yards and Stevie speaks up.

"Why do that, when..." Stevie starts a question and Jamie interrupts him with a hug.

"Shush Stevie," Jamie softly hushes him. He looks at her angrily and shakes away from her.

Before he could reply, Jamie explains softly, "This is a part of the plan, just go along with us." Without saying anymore, Stevie smacks his forehead with his own hand, knowing he had again forgot.

I round the fence, running along the right field fence and look back to The Buddies. They are now swinging on the swings, waiting for me to come back with a flashlight. Stevie was probably going to ask me why go get a flashlight, when we already know what's inside of the cave and we could just go report it to Officer Clifford.

But what Stevie is forgetting is that we need to go through every motion and to act like we had just found a cave for the first time.

Soon back home and in my garage, I get the flashlight I had used before. Barely catching my breath, I run back to the park. Another thing about going back in the cave, is that the cave muck will be on us when we go get Officer Clifford.

Again this all plays out, like we had just discovered the cave for the first time.

Back at the park, The Buddies are up by the dugouts, with a scared look on their faces and looking towards the cave. I hurry around the park entrance and down to the dugouts.

"What's wrong?" I ask, knowing that this wasn't a part of the plan.

Darwin stares across the outfield towards the cave and says, "Someone ran out of the cave."

"What? Who was it?" I couldn't believe what I had heard and look across the field.

"He was wearing black clothes and a black stocking cap," Stevie said, staring and pointing.

"We were swinging and looking towards the road, waiting for you to show up, when we heard the brush rustle and we looked over to see a dark figure run through the brush and up and over the bank," Jamie replies. Each of The Buddies look scared and still looking over at the cave.

"Do you guys know who it could be?" I ask, as I walk slowly along the fence. The others are hesitant to follow me. Their fear holds them back, but slowly they follow.

"No. I don't have a clue," Jamie said, "The person was running fast."

"No... I suppose it could be one of the town hoods. I don't really know." Darwin replies.

"I'm scared. What if he comes back?" Stevie said, holding back my arm.

"I don't think they will, because they don't want to be discovered, and be tied to the money and the skeleton," I reply and try to console Stevie.

"Oh, I don't know Lucas. I'll wait right here for you guys." He said, too scared to go on.

"All right, wait for us and we'll be right out." I said, as Stevie steps up to the fence. Along the back side of the out field fence we walk. We strain to see anyone who might be in the trees and brush.

Darwin is uneasy about going inside the cave. Even more so than waiting outside of the cave. "I'll wait out here for you guys to come back out. I mean, I don't need to go in there, do I?"

"No, you don't have to. Jamie and I will be right back out. You can wait over by the swings with Stevie," I reply. Jamie and I are ready to go look inside, like we have never been inside before. "Jamie. Look at the mucky foot prints here." On the patchy grass and dirt, blotches of cave muck show a foot pattern.

"See, this is the proof and they're heading south," Jamie says, pointing to each print until it fades away into the brush.

I place my size eight tennis shoe next to the first print. "It looks to be about a size nine or ten," I think.

"Good work Sherlock," Jamie said and smiles. Darwin is back with Stevie, as Jamie and I inch our way through the opening. The tree roots and vines try to block our path, as we fight on through. Jamie shines the light, as I follow closely behind.

"Hey Jamie. The person you guys saw, must have been small in size, otherwise they wouldn't fit in here. And with a size ten shoe, they must be just a little bigger than I am."

Jamie stops in a crouching position and turns to ask, "Have you been watching the Hardy Boys on television?" The glow of the flashlight, highlights her face.

I snicker and reply, "Some of their shows. I guess it's in the details."

"So someone else has an interest in your discovery," Jamie said and pauses to think.

"Yeah, I thought I really had found a treasure. Now someone else knows about this."

"You think they took the money?" Jamie softly asks, as if someone was listening.

"I don't know. There must be something going on here." I reply in a whisper.

Further inside, we were able to stand up. Jamie and I slowly walk on towards the skeleton and money, watching our steps. The bats are fluttering and squeaking above us.

At the skeleton, still covered with the plastic, Jamie holds the light while I move the plastic cover. The skeleton is still in the same position as we left it. Jamie makes a grimacing sound as the light shines on the gruesome sight.. I cover it up and check the money bag, and something wasn't right.

Jamie shines the light inside of the bag and I notice that the bills was not where we had left them. I look up to Jamie and she looks back. With the bag secured and stashed back, Jamie asks, "How much money do you think is there?"

"I suppose it could be thousands." I reply as I cover up the bag. "Let's get going." Jamie and I carefully head on out, checking first to see if the coast is clear. All seems to be clear as we work our way out. I help Jamie out and we both wipe off some of the muck.

"Do we say anything about the dark person?" Jamie asks quietly.

"Hum.... I don't know. Let me think about it. Lets go find Darwin and Stevie."

Jamie and I walk on towards the right field fence. Darwin and Stevie rushes around to meet us. "Is everything the same as you left it?" Darwin asks.

"Not exactly. Let's go sit in the dugout." I reply, and we all head to the first base dugout. Quickly we go through the fence and into the dugout.

"Is the money still there?" Stevie quickly asks, and squirms on the bench in anticipation.

"Shush... Yes, but not like we had left it. I think some may be gone." I said quietly.

"The money inside of the bag was moved, because the bills was not how we left it," Jamie whispers.

"That suspicious person must have taken some of it," Darwin said quietly, leaning in to The Buddies for a group reply.

"Could have. This is what we will need to do. We'll explain the discovery and the mysterious dark person to Officer Clifford. Because if we don't, we could be in trouble for withholding valuable information from the authorities." I explain the best solution to this twist of event.

"Oh yeah. And that man could be the killer of the skeleton or involved somehow," Darwin said quietly and looks around nervously. The Buddies all look around, scared of the mysterious scene.

"All right. That man or person wouldn't dare come forward, in fear of being involved with a death or crime of some sort. Listen now, we'll stay here and Stevie... do you know where the police office is at downtown?" I ask him.

"Yes. Right next to the Library." He said excitingly. Stevie acting eager to do something great.

"The Buddies need you to run downtown, find Officer Clifford and tell him we need him at the park. It's very important. We'll wait right here," I said.

"I can do it!" Stevie said, and hops down. "My red ball jets are fast. I'll be right back, code three." Out of the dugout Stevie runs.

"No need to say anything else," I said, peering out. Stevie waves as he leaves a dusty trail.

The Buddies sit still, looking out across the ball field, over towards the hidden cave. Nothing else is seen, nothing unusual. We talk about who the suspect could be and why they would be involved with the cave, the skeleton and the money. And why wasn't it reported before now? There are a lot of speculations among us.

Before long, a car pulls into the park lot and Jamie says, "It's Officer Clifford."

That was quick. We step on out to go meet Officer Clifford and Stevie, as they get out of the car. "I found him!" Stevie said.

Officer Clifford says, "Hello guys and gal. What's this about a cave, skeleton, a money bag and a dark mysterious person?" He has a clip board and jots down something.

He is wearing dark blue pants, nice shiny black shoes and light blue shirt with patches and a badge. His dark brown hair is combed back and his sunglasses has mirror-like lenses. On his right side is a black gun holster, with a big black gun.

"From here you can't see it, but to the right of the swings is the hidden cave," I explain.

He looks at the muck on Jamie and myself and asks if we were mud wrestling, and laughs.

"Where did this mysterious person go to?" He asks, looking towards the swings. Darwin explains that up through the trees, brush and over the bank they went.

Clifford writes down more information. "Let me get the camera to take some pictures," he said, going to the truck of his car. He asks what we were doing at the park today, what we were doing when we first found the cave and for any other details.

I said, "We were just swinging on the swings, when I noticed a dark area in the brush and went to see what it was. Behind the small trees and brush, I pulled apart the roots and vines to see a gap, large enough to get into. But the opening was too dark, so I ran home to get my flashlight." He sees that the flashlight I am holding is also mucky. As we talk, Clifford keeps writing.

He is nice to us as always, even cuts up a little bit. That's why all the kids like him. He knows all of us and knows how to talk to us. "Let's go over to take some pictures," He said. All of us walk side by side, feeling safe now that Officer Clifford is here.

CHAPTER THIRTEEN

Authorities Come To Town

Officer Clifford gets on his car radio, dials in a channel and places a call, "Unit 169 to DNR 105." He glances and cracks a smile to us. Then gives The Buddies a thumbs-up sign.

A static deep-voice replies, "This is DNR 105, go ahead."

"Can you meet me at the Summer Set town park for a signal 76?" Officer Clifford asks.

We look at each other, and wonder what is a signal 76? "I can be there in about 32 minutes," the deep-voice replies. We stand by the squad car, talking and even glance across the ball field to again watch over the scene. Darwin, Jamie and Stevie act calm during our conversation.

"Clear. We will be standing by," replies Clifford, and hangs up his microphone.

"Clear," called the deep voice again on the radio. I can visualize a large officer with a smoky-the-bear hat coming to the park.

"All right," Officer Clifford said to us, "We'll wait right here, but I need to write down your names, addresses and phone numbers," as he gets his clip board out.

Each of us give our information and then he asks, "To help secure the scene, do you guys

want to help me?"

"Sure," we all reply, happy to help Officer Clifford out. But I just had to ask, "What is a signal 76?"

"Signal 76 is a possible death discovery." He goes to the rear of his car and out of the trunk, he gets a large roll of yellow police tape. "You say there is a skeleton inside the cave?"

"Yes," said Jamie. The Buddies together, watches Officer Clifford work the course of the law. A car pulls into the ball park's parking lot, its Stevie's Father.

"Oh no. I'll be right back, guys," said Stevie, as he hesitates to leave. Officer Clifford leads us back to the cave, while Stevie talks to his Father at the car. Officer Clifford explains that since this is a death scene, we'll need to secure this area and it would unlawful to cross the yellow police tape.

"Wow. Just like they do on television, a crime scene," Darwin said excitingly. Officer Clifford ties one end of the tape to a strong bush on the hillside, a few yards from the cave opening, and then walks around a small tree. As we walk together, he has us stay outside of the yellow tape.

Around another small tree we walk and towards a bush, as the yellow tape leads us.

To another bush up on the hillside, across the top around trees and back down to where we had started.. The taped off area is about thirty feet across and all across the tape, it says, 'POLICE LINE - DO NOT CROSS.'

Stevie then runs up to us, while his Father is still sitting in the car watching us.

"I have to leave here in a few minutes." Stevie said.

Officer Clifford explains that there is nothing we can do now and we can go on home if we want to.

Although each one of us may be called to meet with an Officer of the law to discuss what we had found and what we had seen and did.

The Buddies agree and tell Officer Clifford goodbye. And we would see him again soon. We did ask one last question about discussing this with anyone. He said that he would prefer we didn't, as we would probably be called this afternoon or evening to testify. He explains that we need to tell the authorities the truth to the questions.

As we walk away, another car pulls into the lot. A man gets out and talks to Stevie's Father. They point and look over towards the yellow tape. Up by the road are some ladies walking by and they too are alerted to the scene. Over by the park's entrance, Tony Watson and his hoods ride by on their bikes. They go on by, but soon slow and stop, looking over also. We get over by Stevie's car and his Father wants to talk to Stevie, so we said goodbye and will see Stevie later.

Tony Watson and his friends ride back to the park entrance and roll on in. As we walk on to leave, Tony asks, "What did you guys do now? You're all muddy. What happened?"

"Nothing. We were just playing. They think they've found something," I reply, not wanting to tell them anything.

"What? A dead body," ask one of his friends and then they all laugh.

I said, "That's a good one." Tony and his goons like to wear ragged dark clothes.

They ride on down to the dugouts. That dead body answer shocked me as being suspicious.

We glance at each other and then look back to them, as they coast down to the dugouts. As we walk up to the sidewalk to go home, Jamie's Mother drives up to us from behind.

She of course wants to know what was going on, as more town people walk to the park to also see what was going on. News travels fast in a small town.

Jamie's Mother was going to give all of us a ride home, but because we were all mucky, she didn't want us in her car.

She told Jamie to get home right away to get cleaned up, so they could talk. Then a DNR car drives up and into the park. An officer puts on a smoky-the-bear hat and then gets out. A large man, just as I had thought, stands straight and tall in his army green pressed uniform.

His sharp uniform with badges and patches on it makes me a little nervous. He walks on around the dugout as Officer Clifford meets him as they shake hands.

The teen hoods and other people, who have gathered, stand still to watch them. The two Officers talk a little and then walk on over to the yellow tape. A small crowd stands near the ball park fence watching, as this is the most excitement that has hit this town since a few years ago, when some man caught a forty pound lake catfish out of the reservoir.

More town people are either driving or walking to the park as the word must be raging across the town like wildfire. We stand up on the sidewalk which overlooks the ballpark to watch the scene grow larger, some little kids are even playing in the ball diamond and some older kids in our classes are swinging on the swings. People are funny. This sleepy little town is coming awake and fast.

"We better go home to get cleaned up, I feel we'll soon be called to testify and I want to see what happens next at the cave," Darwin said. We all agree and start for home. We also said that we will meet right back here in an hour.

After a nice warm shower and some lunch, I hurry on back to the park. Mother wasn't home yet and Father is at work. They will be totally surprised of the discovery and scared that we went into a cave. At the end of my street, I round the corner to look down towards the park.

A sight never seen here are that both sides of the street are packed with cars all lined up. People are crossing the street and walking on the sidewalks like there was a street fair going on.

Out of breath from running, I arrive to the upper sidewalk overlooking the ball park. The sound of everyone talking, some laughing, and some babies crying, makes me kind of scared.

Many people are shoulder to shoulder at the fence and packed so deep, I had to go out around. Darwin and Jamie are probably here somewhere, as I look around for them. This is the biggest thing I have ever seen here in this town.

Through to the fence I worm my way, where The Buddies had agreed we would meet, as I look across to the cave. There are many officials of the law working around the yellow tape, going in out of the taped-off boundary. A few officers are studying the mucky footprints going up into the hillside brush. There by the cave is a smaller official, who works his way into the cave with the help of the DNR Officer who came earlier when we were here.

People around me are talking of how no one has never noticed the cave being there before. Someone even spoke that the hillside cave opened up due to a small earthquake we had. But I don't remember hearing about an earthquake.

Another person could be heard saying the rains we recently had, washed out the opening. Oh Boy! The things people will talk about. I didn't say a word.

Around the area I look, but don't see my Buddies. The ball diamond is full of kids running around. The swings congested with older kids, some adults including some town council members are near the yellow boundary tape. Many people are around taking pictures of the scene, some people are even up on the cliff taking pictures.

The whole park seems congested with people talking, coming and going.

Darwin and Jamie must be around here somewhere, so I weasel my way back out and work down the busy drive to the park. I know most of the people here or know that they live around the area. Many say hello and some ask me about the discovery. I just down-play it, not saying what I really know.

There by the dugout, Darwin and Jamie is talking to some kids in our class. The parking lot is been cleared of public cars by the officials, so law enforcement vehicles could work the scene.

A squad car has the park entrance blocked off, with its emergency lights flashing. I didn't know this many people even lived around here. People are sitting on the bleachers talking and watching. The dugouts are even full, mostly of kids.

Finally I get to The Buddies and we talk with other classmates around. Our classmates can't believe this special occurrence has happen. The Buddies never let on, probably afraid of being mobbed with questions and answers. I know the story will be let out and this will be all over the newspapers, but right now, I'm not ready.

We stand by, watching the officials work the scene, taking pictures and measurements. They seem to be writing a lot of information down. A small man comes out of the cave covered with muck. He talks to some officials and they in-turn talk on radios and special telephones.

A car marked 'Army Corp of Engineers' is allowed to drive in and two men get out with a camera bag and notebook. They walk over and talk to some Officers and then take notes and some pictures.

"Wow," said Jamie, "I didn't know this was going to be such a big thing."

I whisper in Jamie's ear, "Guess since there is a big discovery with a skeleton and money bag, they'll call in everyone that is needed." Some kid jumps on my back and laughs. I turn to see that its Stevie, "Hey Stevie, where have you been?"

"I had to go eat some lunch and explain what happened," said Stevie, then he realizes that others nearby could have heard him. Then he acted confused and said, "I didn't know."

Officer Clifford then came up to us and said, "Can I talk to you guys." The Buddies went with him over to his car, away from the crowd and anyone who could hear us.

"We need each of you to go get your parents and come downtown for a short meeting with myself and the DNR Officer. I'll see each of you in an hour," Officer Clifford said.

All of us agree and we leave as several people look at us like we are front page news. I feel very uncomfortable and Stevie whispers to me about the death-pact wish.

I said to Stevie in a whisper, "It's all clear now. We kept our pact to the end, Officer Clifford was the one to report to." As we walk out around the crowd standing on the sidewalk, a car screeches its brakes to avoid hitting us.

We jump back and Darwin shouts, "Whoa. That was close." We run across the street to get away from the crowd. People are still watching us walk away.

"Are you sure we're clear of the death-pact wish?" Stevie said, "That was a close one."

"Yes. I'm sure. Let's get home to tell our parents of the meeting," I said.

"What do you think they will ask us?" asks Darwin, who seems concerned of our meeting.

"They will probably ask each of us, how we came to find the cave and why did we explore it by ourselves. Maybe even what we had found inside and what we did when we found the skeleton and the money bag," I said.

"Just remember what we had agreed upon and how I accidently found the cave over by the swings." I then hush, as people pass us, probably going to the park after hearing of the exciting news. We soon leave each other and will see each other at the police department downtown.

After finding my Mother and a quick explanation, we drive on to the downtown office. Father won't be able to be there, he has a hard time getting off of work. I overheard her talking to Dad, something about she could handle it without him and she told him 'Thanks.'

We couldn't drive pass the park due to the congestion, so we drove around several blocks to reach downtown. At the police station, Mother parks the car and we go on in.

We were told to wait in the lobby, as each of us would be called to testify. A sheriff deputy sits with us, probably so we don't talk about the case. He did explain that each one of us, one by one would go in with our parents. And as each one would come out from testifying, we were to leave the station without talking. I guess it's so we don't talk to the others about what we had talked about.

It was my turn first, Mother and I went in. We sit at a small round table. Officer Clifford asks if it was all right to record the meeting. Mother and I agree it was okay. He then introduces us to Mr. Darren Asborne, the DNR Officer over this county. He has a stern look on his face as he shakes our hands. The lines on his weathered face shows many years of being out in the field and on the water.

Another person in the room is a county sheriff to which I have never seen before. He is introduced as Officer James Clark and he also shakes our hands.

Officer Clifford first starts by asking me, "What were the Buddies doing this morning at the park?" The other two officials are writing down some information.

I explain, "I have been busy helping my brother mow yards and paint for the past three days, and I really needed to go with my friends to the cliffs and the park to play this day. To relax and to just have fun. School will be starting soon and summer will be over."

Officer Asborne asks, "How did you happen to find the cave entrance?"

I said, "We were playing on the swings when I looked over and saw something dark in the hillside brush. I went over, with my friends asking me where I was going, to the tree roots and vines and there it was."

"Then what did you do?" The Sheriff asks. The other officers continue to write with a tape recorder rolling. I thought while watching the reels of the recorder spin.

"The dark opening was covered by the vines and roots. So I pulled them apart to look and told the others that I needed to go home to get a flashlight. They said they would wait for me, as I ran home and then came right back."

"Were you scared and did you tell anyone about the cave before you went in to explore it?" Asks Officer Clifford.

As I shift in my seat and look at Mother, I said, "Yeah, a little bit I suppose... but I've been spelunking before in the Boy Scouts. So it was fun and exciting to find a cave."

"How long have you been a Boy Scout and how many caves have you explored?" Officer Asborne asks.

"I was a Cub Scout first for two years and then became a Boy Scout and have been for almost a year now. I have probably been on about four cave trips with my troop." I said.

"While in the cave, you saw the skeleton. Did you touch or move the skeleton?" Officer Clifford asks. Mother sits quiet and look at me after each question as she twiddles her fingers.

"The only thing that happened was that I accidently tripped over the skeleton, because it was

dark in there and I was watching the bats. Then I peeked under the plastic cover to see that it was a human skeleton. The first sight of it, did startle me."

"The money bag was under the cover with the skeleton, did you touch the money?" Asks Officer James Clark.

"Yes, I didn't know what it was until I opened the bag and seen there were bundles of money. I may have flipped through the bundles to see what the bills were... I suppose... But I didn't bother them. My first thought was, that this discovery needs to be reported to Officer Clifford."

"The dark suspect that left the cave, do you have a clue as to whom it may be?" Asks Officer Clark.

"No, not right now," I thought and then said, "I may have to think about it."

There were no immediate questions and they finished writing. Officer Clifford then asks the others if they have any more questions and they said, 'No'. "Very good Lucas," said Officer Clifford and shook my hand, then my Mother's hand. "We hope this wasn't too hard of a meeting for you. If you think of anything else that is important, please get back with us." The other Officers also shook our hands with a smile.

"We may need to contact you if there is anything else," said Officer Asborne.

"That'll be fine. If I can help solve this case, I would be happy to do so," I said.

"People may ask you about what is going on, and it would be best if you would just say 'It's an on-going case and you're not entitled to say," said Officer Clark.

"All right," I reply and we all say goodbye. Officer Clifford leads us out the door and as we pass the others waiting, they look at me with a concern look on their faces.

With a smile, I give them a thumb-up sign. As we went out the door, I hear them ask Stevie and his parents to come on in. In the car, Mother said, "That was interesting," and she pats my thigh. "Its amazing that something like this happen so close to home.

I mean the cave alone is something, but a human skeleton and a money bag is really something."

"Yeah. Guess I was in the right place at the right time." I wanted to tell Mother everything, but couldn't. I feel that the one secret The Buddies have is the one at twenty-five feet under water. Maybe someday The Buddies will explore it together as certified divers.

"I wonder who the skeleton actually is? I don't know of any missing persons. What's odd is the bag of money.

How much money do you think is in it?" Mother asks, she seems to be excited over the mystery and before I could answer. "And are there any markings on the bag?"

"I don't know who it could be. The money... could be a thousand dollars or more. There aren't any markings, I could see on the bag." I drop my head to think, so much to think about. How can this happen to me in this little town? Or is it my own destiny?

"Oh wow!" said Mother, looking over the steering wheel. There in front of us is a crowd of people gathered by the park. "I guess I should have driven the other way."

"Why did you come this way, Mom?" I said, concerned we may be trapped. Afraid that the word may get around that I made a discovery and what kind of reception would I face.

"I was curious and wanted to see what was going on." Mother slowly drives through the crowd as they move out of the way and many recognize us, saying, 'There's Lucas,' and 'He's the one who found the cave,' and, 'Hello Lucas, our Hometown Hero.'

"You want me to stop so you can talk to your fans?" Mother asks, as I wave to them.

"No, I don't know if I'm ready yet. I don't really know about all of this."

"I don't think it will be so bad. People around here know you anyway and they'll be nice."

"Yeah. But I'd rather wait for The Buddies, to see what they thought of the meeting. Let's go on home."

Mother seems to understand as she finally clears the congestion to head on home. Back home, I try to relax, get something to drink and start to watch some television. But the telephone rings and Mother answers it, someone she knows asking about what happened at the park. I hear her explain and then say that I'm fine, but resting now.

She hangs up and starts to tell me who it was, when the telephone rings again. We know so many people and they all mean well, but this is crazy.

Mother is now talking to this caller about the cave. Ooh, I can't relax here. I'm going to the park and face the music.

Mother is still talking about the excitement, as I walk by to interrupt her, saying "I'm going to the park. I'll be home in a few hours." She waves 'Okay,' and keeps on talking.

I may as well face the crowd. The news is probably in the next county by now. The Buddies should be coming home by now, I just hope they keep it all together and stay calm. They've all been good at keeping secrets, but if under any pressure... I'm not sure.

"Hey Lucas! I heard you found a wonderful surprise today," Mr. Thomas said from a side yard at the end of our street. He startled me as my mind was thinking about the authorities.

"Yeah, it really surprised me too," I reply and keep on walking. The crowd doesn't seem as large as it was before. They're all standing along the fence, overlooking the park.

CHAPTER FOURTEEN

The Investigation

An hour must have passed since they took away the mummy and other items. The few remaining officers talk and wait by their vehicles. Many bystanders have left and a few kids are playing as their parents mingle in small groups. On the bleachers are some elders visiting with each other.

Everyone here has an opinion as to what happened and who the skeleton might be and about the bag of money. I just listen and don't say much as I really don't know. "Lucas, what's going on?" Asks James from behind me, again his voice startles me. Everyone nearby turns to look and some knows James well. "Mother said you found a cave and a body."

"Yeah, it's over there by the swings," I reply and point out across the ball field. The others standing beside us, tells James that he has a celebrity as a brother and that I am a town hero.

James smiles and makes a remark which I didn't hear. Around people he curbs his attitude and shows people what they want to see and hear.

"Hey Lucas!" Shouts Darwin from down the sidewalk. Jamie and him wave and run towards us, probably coming from their homes. I wave back, then leave the bystanders to go meet them.

We meet away from the crowd to discuss what was said at the police department. Stevie couldn't come out, as his parents are leery about him coming back down here alone. No one could hear us quietly talk. Darwin and Jamie said that they were asked questions about how I happen to find the cave? What we did when the dark stranger ran from the cave? Whom we think the stranger is? What did we then do, and why did we decide to go in the cave? Also what did we do with the skeleton and the money?

The Buddies seem to have all answered the questions about the same. I ask if they felt Stevie had answered the same as we did and they had already asked him. They said that he had said he did and stayed true to the plan, just as we all have done.

Over by the blocked park entrance, a vehicle pulls up and a young woman and a man get out to talk to the Officer. They all look towards our direction and we are then called over to the officer. What could be happening now? We wonder what's up as we walk through the remaining people, with their friendly congratulations. We walk nervously up to the requesting officer and the strangers.

"Lucas Lousure?" The young woman asks with a smile and a welcome hand to shake. The man next to her with a camera, snaps some pictures of us.

"Yes," I reply and shake her hand, but wonder what this is all about. The Buddies stand together beside me, probably also wondering.

"I am Nicole Richmar from the Wabash Herald newspaper and we would like to do a story and take some photos," she asks, "Could we get your parents to give consent to this story?"

The photographer takes more photos from a different angle. "Uh... Yeah, I think they would," I said with hesitation and then look at Darwin and Jamie. The news lady asks if there is another boy in our group, like she must have heard there was.

We said there is and his name is Stevie Thomas, he lives just a few blocks over there. "Do you think we could get him to come back here for the story?" The news lady asks, "If his parents could give consent and bring him here, that would be great." I said that we could go to his house to get him.

The attending officer spoke up to say he could have dispatch give all of our parents a telephone call, to speed up the wait. We all said that would work. The officer gets on his radio and calls in. After a few questions about the park and the cave from the news lady - the Sheriff dispatch calls back to say that all of the parents will soon be coming to the park.

The Buddies all stand together and then the news lady asks each of us some questions about ourselves. Many bystanders gather around to listen as I look to locate James. He is no where to be seen.

After several minutes, our parents arrive and ask some questions themselves. Stevie and his parents arrive to stop at the guarding Officer, as we talk to Stevie by ourselves.

They all give consent for the news story and request to see the photos before they are to be published. The news lady and photographer comply, then ask more questions and more photos are taken. The news people want some pictures taken over in front of the cave. We all go around the outfield fence to the Officer guarding the cave scene.

Bystanders follow us and some call out our names in support, and many are taking pictures themselves. The news lady asks the officer if they could take some photos in front of the cave and he said to stand on the other side of the yellow tape - and to go no further.

The Buddies stand on the other side of the police line, holding the tape to our waists. The photographer stands about ten feet away and adjusted the angle, he said to be able to get the cave in the background.

Then takes a few pictures and then asks us to kneel down together and takes a few more. Then he asks if we could lay down in the grass, with Darwin and me on the bottom facing the camera and Jamie on top of me and Stevie on top of Darwin. A playful type of photo, again with the cave in the background. We giggle through this shoot and the news lady and photographer is very nice to us. Our parents and the bystanders watching also laughed and cheer us on.

All of this attention is great, but we still feel nervous because of the dark secret we had. The Buddies secret will be kept deep in our hearts. The news people thanks us and tells us the story with photos may be in tomorrow's newspaper. They leave to talk to the guarding officer and asks about the skeleton and the money bag.

His only reply was that the skeleton is at a morgue and tests will be done to try to determine who it could be. The money is being held at a police lab for finger printing and tests. The serial numbers will be researched at a federal reserve bank. No other information can be given at this time.

We start to leave, when an officer says that the Police Lab just called and requests the Buddies to go to the police station to have our finger prints taken.

Our hearts sank as our parents comfort us and questions the officer about this Lab request.

The officer said its only to verify whose prints are whose and to see if there are prints that are suspicious. We leave the park with our parents, to go downtown again - a feeling like one would be in trouble and have to go to the principles office.

In the police station, each one of us leaves a set of finger prints. "I feel like a criminal," said Stevie, as his parents hug and assure him that its all right. A few of our Fathers ask the officers some questions about the investigation. And our Mothers remind us that we just happen to find the cave and inside, the skeleton and the money.

"Yeah, we did. And we didn't take any of the money. Because it didn't belong to us and I *knew* we had to report this to Officer Clifford," I said to an officer, as The Buddies look stone-faced and sit, wiping their forefingers with rubbing alcohol to remove the black ink. Officer Clifford walks through the front door with open arms, just like he's one of us.

"Don't worry my friends, this is only to see if there are any unidentifiable prints. Maybe we can trace a print to the dark stranger who ran from the cave," Officer Clifford said, "Or whom the skeleton may be." Officer Clifford is always nice to all of us.

We're happy the town hired him a few years ago. "We just received a special report from the DNR. They have found that the bats using the cave, are rare Indiana Bats and that they *must* not be disturbed." He explains, "They are planning to somehow secure the cave and will take action soon."

We all look at each other in awe and then one parent says, "It must be sealed, so kids can't get in there."

Officer Clifford explain that the DNR won't seal up the entrance completely, but it will be secured somehow and will be guarded until the work is completed. He asks us to be thinking about who the dark suspect could be. As we leave the station, he said he would be in contact with us soon.

On the way home, we drive by the park to see what was happening now. Bystanders are still over-looking the park and the DNR are working around the boundary, doing some construction work. "Oh wow. Officer Clifford was right," I said, "Gosh... Now there's a State police car."

Officer Clifford didn't say anything about the State police being here.

"Maybe they felt like they need to assist. This is really something, Lucas. People will never forget this, as your name will go down in the town history." I never thought of that. Remembered as the boy who found a cave, skeleton and a bag full of money.

But now there is a dark suspect who ran from the cave and Officer Clifford wants us to help find who it could be. Although it would be hard to mention to the law whom I think Iit could be. There are a few in mind... but it's an awful thought. I need to discuss this with The Buddies.

I want to talk to Mother about what I think, but I'm afraid to. All evening, Mother talks about the discovery, as she never had a chance before. The story retold as it was reported to the officials, nothing else. Same again when Father came home. The discussion went on and on.

Soon I was on the telephone to The Buddies, to meet again tomorrow at the cliffs. We need to put our heads together on whom it could be. Maybe they have the same name ideas as I do. They all said ten o'clock in the morning would be all right.

The following day, I got a notepad and four pencils from my room and start for the door. "Lucas, where you going this morning?" Mother asks, as I pause at the door.

"The Buddies has some work to do on a project. I'll be home in a few hours."

"Listen, if this project has something to do with the police scene, just be smart and careful."

"All right Mother, thanks. I'll be back soon." Out the door and down the sidewalk I rush on. Mother does support me and my ideas, and she means well. She is a better person than what my father is. I just wish he would spend more time with us. His job really has him consumed. Yeah, he makes very good money... but is it worth it?

Near the park, some elders stand talking quietly to each other. They must be watching some action going on. Closer now, I can see the DNR working the scene. They have large black iron fence posts in the ground and some huge black fence panels in place.

Other workers are loading up a concrete mixer and other tools into a trailer. Over in the parking lot is a sheriff's car. I stand and watch the work going on, when The Buddies call out my name from far down the sidewalk, "Hey Lucas!"

Darwin, Jamie and Stevie hurry towards me as the bystanders briefly watch us. We quietly talk and then walk on around to the parking lot. The sun glare on the windshield of the sheriff's car wouldn't let me see who the sheriff is. As we walk on by, the sheriff glances at us and flips his hand to say hello. We keep on walking towards the trail, glancing over at the scene, being built up like a medieval fortress. The iron panels look to be eight feet tall, to keep even mischievous kids out.

"That is something. I guess they don't want anyone going near the cave," Jamie said.

"I have never seen anything like this around here before," Darwin replies and look back.

"Wholly cow! This is wonderful, we could be crowned heroes," Stevie said excitingly.

"I didn't think all of this excitement would come out of the cave. Guess it's really a big deal," I said, as we reach the top of the cliff and to see a favorite view of mine. The sun shining bright reflects off of the reservoir. The tree rope flutters in the breeze enticing us to jump on for a swinging good time.

But not this time, maybe later today. A white sailboat in the distance catches a full sail of wind while slicing through the waters. We settle down under the oak tree and I give everyone a sheet of paper and a pencil.

"Each of us may have thoughts as to whom we feel the dark suspect could be. Write down the possible suspects and don't say a word," I said.

"I think my..." Stevie starts to say, as I quickly look up to interrupt him.

"Shush. Just write down your thoughts and fold your paper," I said quickly. "It's your secret, and no one, not even your Buddies need to know who you think is the suspect. Because a name could upset any of us." The Buddies think and write, then put their folded paper in the envelope and then I sealed it.

"Anyone who fits the description, could be a suspect and with some other clues each of us may already know about," I said.

"I could think of a few suspects myself," Jamie sadly said, drawing in the dirt with her pencil.

"I wrote down four names myself," said Darwin, reaching out to hand me his pencil.

"I'm sad to have written down some names too," Stevie said, tossing his pencil to me.

"Sad?" I ask, picking up the pencil and having an idea as to what Stevie is saying.

"Yeah, sad to think a person could be involved in a crime. A person who has a loving Mother," said Stevie, doodling in the dirt.

"Yeah, it's probably someone we know," Darwin said, looking at each of us with a straight face.

"Come on guys. Let's go find Officer Clifford and give him this envelope," I said, wanting to stop this sad discussion, and hopping up on my feet.

Down the trail we walk, brushing dirt off of our pants. We quietly walk not saying a word. The DNR are still erecting black iron fence panels to the posts while an officer stands nearby, talking to a Conservation Officer.

A State police car is in the lot with two Officers leaning against it. Some business men from downtown are talking to the officers. Little kids are playing in the park like they never have before, their parents are watching close by.

The summer heat today would have us cooling off in the waters below the cliff. But with this big event going on, none of The Buddies even mention it. Our normal routine is put on hold for a while. We walk past the State police car as the four men stop talking and watch us go on by. It's as if everyone now knows that we are the explorers who had found the discovery.

Bystanders still watch from the bleachers and the upper sidewalk. At the park entrance a lady says, "Smile," and takes our picture with a large camera. The flash nearly blinds us as we stand surprised. She introduces herself as a news reporter from the Marion Tribune newspaper. She asks us questions for the news and we told her our story. The same story we had given the Wabash news and the Law Officials. Another picture was taken before we went on towards town.

"I don't know if I like all of this attention," Jamie said, as she looks around.

"Maybe we should ask Officer Clifford about all of this," said Darwin. As we reach the downtown area, across the corner at the gas station, were some teenagers getting gas.

One of them yells out to us, "Hey, our heroes!" Another one shouts, "Can we have your autograph?" Then they laugh and ask us to come on over.

We hurry on into the police station. Officer Clifford is talking on the telephone, as we sit to wait our turn. We over hear him say, "Yes, we're aware of it... No... it has not been made public yet."

He looks at us and smile. "No, the park will be safe when the DNR is finished. I need to go now. Have a nice day." He hangs up and shakes his head. "What can I do for you guys?" He asks nicely.

"We secretly made out suggestions as to whom we feel is the dark suspect. They're in this sealed envelope.

This is so no one gets upset as to whom we suspect," I said, and hands him the envelope. "Do you have any suspects in mind?"

"Thanks. We have only suspicions. What we'll do is take your suggestions and see where to go from here. A full investigation is still going on."

Jamie asks, "We're being asked questions and pictures are taken by reporters for a story. And other people are making comments. Some seem rude. It seems scary to us. What should we do?"

"If you feel uncomfortable or too many questions are thrown at you, you may want to stay near home or have your parents with you while your out."

"Yeah, even some kids are saying things to us," Stevie said.

"We may want to put you into witness protection," Officer Clifford said and then cracks a smile. We all knew he was just kidding and laugh.

He told us to talk to our parents to see if we need to change our public appearances a little bit.

"If you have any other thoughts or problems, please get back with me," he said. We feel better talking to our friend and so we left the station to go on home. As we leave the station, two men in suits were outside of the bank. They're standing next to a black car with tinted windows, talking to the bank president.

As they talk, one of the men writes on a notepad, then they walk to the old Laundromat, which is next to the bank. "What's going on," Stevie asks, as we slowly walk to go on home.

"There's some men talking to the bank president, seems odd... the black car, like from a police crime movie," I said.

"Yeah, that is different and look... there's a state police car parked beside the Laundromat," Darwin said. We watch as we walk along.

Some other people are watching from the gas station and from the five and dime store.

"Must be something with the investigation? Wow, this is big time," Jamie said. We walk on to leave the downtown area. Up ahead we see that the park is still congested. The DNR might still be working on the cave site.

Not wanting to face another question or comment, we cross the street to the other side. This route is the only way to our neighborhood from downtown, without cutting through backyards and jumping over many fences.

As we come upon the park area, we can't see down into the park from the other side of the street. We can only see the trees on the rim of the reservoir.

One person notices us walking by and points, while others look our way. But soon turn to watch the work being done down below.

We decide that we need a fun day back at the cliff to swim, and to just relax. As there is only a month left of summer before school starts again. Monday was the best day, as Sunday will be busy with church and family.

One by one, each of us departs to go on home. We will all be talking to our parents about what we had said to Officer Clifford. Hopefully our parents will understand and have a thought as to how we will go on from here. Our plan is to be at the cliff after lunch on Monday. Maybe by then the community excitement will calm down and the harassment will lighten up.

Back home, I find Mother had come home earlier than I thought she would. I spoke to her about what we did today and she said, "The Buddies did the right thing, going to Officer Clifford with a sealed envelope of suspected names. Can you tell me whom you think it could be?"

"Mom... I really can't say. It's a secret, even with The Buddies, we can't tell each other what we think.

It could be hurtful to anyone and we don't want fingers pointing at us as being a snitch." Mother seem to understand as we talk about how we could prevent any harassment or uncomfortable comments.

She is one whom I can always talk to, about anything... or almost anything. As we talk and get a glass of lemonade, the front door bell rings.

Mother said, "It's the State Police," as she goes to the door. Two officers stand in full uniform and one says, "Yes, Mrs. Lousure.

We have a search warrant to obtain a few swabs of specimens from the shoe soles of James Lousure and Larry Lousure's shoes or boots."

Surprised to hear of such a request, Mother gasps for an answer, "I suppose... Is there a probable suspect here? I need to call my husband first."

"We do have a search warrant, Mrs. Lousure," an officer replies. "May we step inside?"

"Yes, that'll be fine. Just wait right there though," Mother said, while she gets on the phone to call Father at work.

"Mrs. Lousure, we have *a search warrant*," an officer replies, holding out the paper.

"Oh, yes, excuse me. Go right ahead," Mother says, hanging up the telephone.

At the kitchen doorway, I stand watching the two officers stand just inside the door. A black briefcase at the side of one officer, the other addresses me, "Hello Lucas." The other officer also says hello with a hand wave.

"Hello sirs," I reply. Mother asks them to remember that Lucas was the founder of the cave.

"Yes Maim, Lucas is not a part of the investigation. We all ready have his shoe prints and he is clear," an officer said. The other officer gets the briefcase set up, with small tube vials.

With the help of Mother and myself, we lead the officers to pairs of shoes and boots of James and Fathers.

They take two swabs and two vials of each shoe and boot. The vials are marked and then recorded with some lengthily information. Only about 15 minutes were needed, and the two officers thank us for our cooperation in this investigation.

"Thank you also. Please excuse my delay, as I wasn't thinking," Mother said, "So these swabs will show what type of bacteria is on the shoes?"

"That's correct, Mrs. Lousure. If you have any thing else that might be of interest to us, please contact the office downtown." The officers said and slowly back out of the door. Their friendly smiles and gentle manners made us feel at ease.

With the officers gone, Mother said, "Ugh, that was scary, but I guess it's okay."

"Yeah, I'm sure it's okay," I said, but really feel uneasy about it.

CHAPTER FIFTEEN

The Case Goes Cold

We were getting ready for the day when there came a ring at the front door. Our Mother goes to the door and says, "It's a County Sheriff's car, again." James looks from the open refrigerator, and I look around the corner towards the front door. "Hello," Mother says the officers.

James and I listen closely. "Good Morning Mrs. Lousure. I'm Gary Donaldson from the Sheriff department. Is Mr. Lousure home?" A manly voice asks from outside of the door.

"No. He's already left for work," She replies. James shrugs and sits at the table.

"All right. I need to ask him some questions. What time does he normally get home from work?" The officer asks. Last night two officers took their samples, what could be left to do?

"He usually gets home about six o'clock," She said, "Can I leave him a message?"

"Yes. You can tell him I'll be back after six to have a talk with him."

"All right, I'll let him know. Have a nice day."

"Thank you Maim. Have a good day." The door closes and Mother walks back to the kitchen.

"That's odd," she says. She gets a refill of hot coffee and sits down. "I wonder if they really suspect your Dad of being involved in the cave case."

"Uh, I don't know Mom. There may be many suspects they'll be talking to," I said.

"Dad does like to go on late evening walks down to the reservoir," James said with a mouth full. Breakfast tastes good, but with this discussion, I soon felt like I've had enough.

"That doesn't sound like your Dad," Mother said, staring down into the table and nibbles at a piece of bacon. She looks to be in deep concentration, probably thinking about Dad. "Although, they did take sample swabs from the shoes and boots."

"What?" Replies James, with a surprised look. Mother and I look up at James.

"Yeah, the State Police came yesterday and with a search warrant, took samples from the bottom of your and Fathers shoes and boots," Mother said.

"So they suspect me and Dad," James snickers, "Don't worry, Mom. I'm sure Dad didn't do it." He said, "It might be old man Johnson. He's always walking among the trees looking for mushrooms, or as he says." Now that's a name I would have never suspected. Mr. Johnson likes to hunt for Indiana mushrooms. There are a lot of people who like to hunt them, although I think James is wrong.

Because it's too late in the season for the morel mushrooms. "Love you Mom. I got a mowing job. Later." He rushes out the door.

"Yeah, I don't think Dad is involved," I said.

Although Dad does have muddy shoes in the corner of the garage. Secretly, I believe Dad might be a suspect, but I don't want to tell Mom that, it could really get her upset. "Mom, so a different type of bacteria or just plain mud, would determine what? Where the shoe had been?"

"The officer said something about the difference between hog, chicken, or bat poop, or again just mud... like river bacteria. Something like that. Finish your milk, we're going shopping today for school clothes."

"Oh, I forgot about that." Today, I did agree to go with her. "How long will we be gone?"

"Only a few hours, why do you ask?"

"I want to go to the park and play around the cliffs."

"Do you ever get tired of going down there?"

"No. We have so much fun there and now, I feel like I'm part-owner of the park."

She laughs and says, "Yes, I'm sure you do and you should be honored."

"Besides, there are only a month left before we have to go to school. Summer will be over before we know it."

"Very fast," I said, with the last drop of milk gone. "I'm ready if you are, Mom?" With the table cleared of breakfast, we leave to go shopping up in Ft. Wayne.

The morning was warm, but mostly cloudy. As we drive by the park, it certainly has become an attraction site. There again are people gathered in the park, mostly around the taped off cave area. A sheriff deputy is guarding the area. None of my Buddies are here. Some kids are playing nearby on the swings and on the ball field. Usually no one would come to the park for days.

Ft. Wayne is a large city in Northeastern Indiana. After an half-hour drive and a few hours of finding several shirts and pants for school, we head for home. After a brief stop for lunch, we are back home just after noon.

Darwin was on the answering machine. He wants me to give him a call as soon as possible. In my bedroom, I gave him a call at home.

"Lucas. Meet me at the cliffs right away," Darwin said in a quick loud whisper.

"What's going on?" I ask. Darwin has never spoken like this before, something is up.

"Meet me there right away." He said and hangs up before I could reply.

Out of my room, I said to Mother, "I'll be home in a few hours, Mom." With my towel, I go through the garage to get my bike. Down the road I pedal fast, with my towel around my neck. I race past the cars in the park's lot, and up the trail to the cliff. My dirt bike wheels spin to get traction, as another bike pedals from behind me. It was Darwin, who is catching up to me. "Hey Buddy," I said with my neck wrenched to see him struggle up the trail.

"Lucas," Darwin replies as he pumps the pedals standing up. We soon disappear into the trees. The Buddies special place is one where we feel safe and free. Where we can have fun and if needed, to talk about our feelings.

There is no one else here, no other Buddies, no other kids and no fishermen down below. With our bikes tossed aside, Darwin stands right in front me and looks right into my eyes. "Lucas. Did the law come to your house?" He whispers.

I should have known. "Yes, and they even took some swab samples from Dads and James shoes and boots," I quietly said.

Darwin grabs my shoulders to get my attention. "Wow! They took my Dads samples from his boots too. Did they also ask about anyone in particular?"

"Yeah. My Dad. A County Sheriff asked about Dad. He will be back after six to talk to him."

"A Sheriff talked to my Dad too," Darwin whispers, "They must have talked for half an hour."

"What did they talk about?" I could not imagine Darwin's Father being involved.

Although his muddy shoes by the back gate, could make him a suspect.

"I don't know, Father only said that he explained to him, that he was a painter." Darwin's voice cracks in his words. As if he himself has doubts of his Father. "Lucas, do you think it's possible?" There he said it, words of doubt. Just as I have doubts about my own Father. He crouches down to sit on the cliff and I also join him.

"To be honest with you, yes, it's possible. Just like it's possible of my own Father." I hate to have said that, but that's how I feel, as it is possible. "It could be anyone who fits that description." And James is wrong. Mr. Johnson wouldn't fit that description, because he is too heavy. One of his legs wouldn't even fit in the cave.

Although my Father and Darwin's Father could fit inside. "Wow. You're right, it is possible." He whispers and stares into the waters.

"Darwin, there could be a dozen people who could fit the description." I explain as he looks out across the reservoir. "I think it's someone who needs money every once in a while."

From the trail comes a running sound of people. Darwin and I jump to our feet and look back.

Jamie and Stevie appear, both are huffing and puffing.

"We knew you would be at the cliffs," said Stevie, who is out of breath.

"The County Deputies came to Stevie's house wanting to talk to his sister," Jamie said.

"Yeah. They came to our houses too. Guess they have in mind some people they need to talk to," I said, as we stand together, with Stevie hanging on the tree rope. We stare out across the reservoir, but I can only see Law Officials knocking on doors and talking to our families.

"We knew this would happen... the officials coming to talk to our families and friends," Darwin said, and The Buddies all look at each other in disbelief. "So, if I understand this right, the shoes or boots that has bat poop on them, is the prime suspect."

"That's how I understand it too. Like, Tammy will probably have hog manure on her boots."

"Yeah, Dad told the Deputy that Tammy was working out at the Evan's pig farm," Stevie said, "They were going to go talk to her out there. Do you think she could have been involved?"

We all look at each other, "Well... she is just a little bigger than Lucas is. She might be able to fit in the cave," Jamie said, trying to ease the thought into Stevie.

"And she does have muddy boots and dark blue coveralls. But I was always told, she uses them on the pig farm. The officers took a few samples of the muck from her boots. She could be a suspect," Stevie said with some hesitation.

"Isn't the Evans farm just around the bend of the river about a mile from here?" Darwin asks and points to the southwest. Then walks to the cliff's edge and points to the left. We follow him and look, "I think those white buildings through the trees over there is the pig farm."

"I believe you're right," I said. We know a lot of people around *Summer Set*, but not everyone. Never have I been to the Evans pig farm, but I have heard of it.

"A lot of days when the weather is nice, she'll just walk across and along the reservoir to go to work," Stevie said and gesturing a walk with his fingers.

The route Stevie just described is close to the back left side of the cave, maybe a few blocks away. One thing I do know, is that the reservoir has rough boundaries. I would think that walking from here to the Evans farm, would be almost impossible. Although I have never walked that way before. "You guys want to go do something?" I ask The Buddies.

"Yeah, let's go play ball with some of the other kids," Jamie says. That's not what I had in mind, but, we leave the area to go play in the park.

My mind goes back to the reservoir area to the north being not too rough and the tree line boarders the town and personal properties, all the way to the bridge where main street crosses the reservoir. But the south edge has tall cliffs and rugged boundaries and I would think it would be quicker riding a bike on the road, than walking along the reservoir. But maybe Tammy doesn't like to ride a bike.

In the park, some of our classmates are playing kickball on the ball diamond. They call us over to join them and so we did. We usually get into a game someone starts up. Either here in the park, at the school or someone's house.

As we are having fun playing ball, there still are people over at the cave. They stand at the black wrought iron fence talking and looking in at the cave. Some of the kids ask us about the cave and whom we think the skeleton is. We say very little about it.

For an hour we had a great time playing kickball. Then several kids said it was time to go home. So the game ended before it was over and we all leave the park to head home. Some kids still asking about the cave and the bats. One kid asks if we got any of the money.

I said, "No, it wasn't our money and we knew we had to contact Officer Clifford about the discovery." Another kid said he would have taken some of it and not said anything.

Darwin said, "That wouldn't be right and you could be prosecuted for taking some." The kids left saying that they never thought of that happening. Our walk on home was quiet. We knew that officers would be around to talk to family members and our close friends.

After a peanut butter sandwich snack, I did my chores and now looking at some Boy Scout merit badge books. One merit badge I was interested in, was the one on micro-biology.

Last year in school, our teacher showed us how to study micro-organisms, which I found to be interesting. The crime lab looking the muck bacteria must be like micro-biology.

After super around six-thirty, I hear the front doorbell ring. Father answers the door and from my bedroom, I could hear him talking to an officer. The officer asks Father if he knew about the cave before I had discovered it. Father said, "No." Then he asks him if he knew of a missing person around twenty some years ago. Father again said, "Right off the top of my head, I don't remember."

Then he asks Father if he ever knew of a bank robbery around twenty-five years ago. Dad said, "I do remember something about the state bank downtown was robbed around about that time. And if I remember right, no one was convicted in that case." The officer said that was right. He then asks Father about going on late evening walks down to the reservoir. Father said, "Yeah. I like to go out by myself to think and relax."

The officer asks where exactly does he go. Father said, "I walk pass the park, down the cliff and along the shoreline to the right.

Usually I go as far as the bridge and turn around and walk back." There is a pause in the conversation and then the Officer asks Father to come downtown tomorrow to leave a finger print.

He then asks him about the size of his shoes. Father says, "Size 10." And asks Father about his height, weight and waist measurements.

Father said, "5'11", about 180 pounds with a 34" waist." Another pause and then the Officer said, "Thank you Mr. Lousure, please see Officer Clifford downtown in a day or so. Have a good evening."

The door closes and Father is heard walking into the kitchen, asking Mother if she heard all of that conversation. The conversation between them is quiet and garbled.

I try to read my book, but my mind runs through names of people who could be a suspect. There are about eight people that I could think of.

Through the book I slowly finger and become interested again. My parents could still be slightly heard talking about the case. After awhile, James comes home from playing basketball with his friends and the conversation comes up again among the three of them.

Something that normally doesn't happen with Father. Maybe a loving moment came to his head and in the light of the case, he feels like being close, like he never has before. Although James didn't stay in the conversation long. He walks down the hall and goes into his room, closing the door behind him.

In a small three-bedroom home, you can hear almost everything being said. Although Father and Mother talks softly, I couldn't hear every word spoken. Of course I'm so into my reading, maybe I'm not paying attention either.

As I turn over onto my back, my eye catches the clock. It shows almost nine o'clock. Up out of bed, I put the books on my dresser. Out into the hall, I go to the kitchen to get a drink of ice cold water.

Father and Mother is watching TV as I walk on by, Mother asks, "What have you been doing?"

"I was studying my Boy Scout merit badges," I reply, getting a cup of ice water. As I walk by again, I said, "I'm tired and going to get ready for bed."

"Very good, son. How about we go fishing this weekend?" asks Father.

Shocked to hear this, I said, "Yeah, that sounds good," I said, almost spilling my drink.

"That sounds like a plan," Father said, reclining back in his chair giving me a thumbs-up sign.

"Good night," I said, as I turn to go down the hall to my bedroom. Father and Mother both said, 'Good night' in unison.

In the bathroom with my robe, ready to take a shower. My mind is on Father and what he might be thinking about all this. Maybe he isn't guilty and maybe he feels all this happening in his face, is hitting home. And maybe something clicked in his heart, maybe I really do mean something to him.

Out of the shower now and brushing my teeth, or just going through all of the motions, my mind is not on what I'm now doing.

As I go on to my bedroom, I hear Father laughing with Mother over a television show. A laughter which I haven't heard in a long time.

Maybe he really wants to be a real Father and husband again.

Chapter Sixteen

Breaking News

"The weather report is saying its going to be hot and sunny day," says Jamie, "Can you go to the cliff today?"

"Yeah, but I have to mow our yard first. I can be there around noon or so," I said.

Mother puts away some kitchen supplies and then butts into our telephone conversation, saying, "Be sure to also trim, Lucas."

"Okay Mom," I reply, with my hand over the receiver. "All right Jamie, see you then?"

"Yeah, sounds good."

"Okay, Bye." Out the door, I go to check out the yard. To my surprise, the heat is cooking so early this morning, as I walk out in the yard in my bare feet. No dew and no dampness, just warm summer green grass. Back in the house to get ready to mow. Our yard is not very big and I can usually mow it in an hour, but then I'll have to trim, which is another thirty minutes.

Row after row I push on, again my mind is not on mowing, but on the suspects and mostly, what if it is Dad ?

What would they do to him? Dad has a good job, why would he even want to risk it all for some cash?

I would guess to say it is either Tony Watson or Tammy Thomas, or... Is it James? James has a good business mowing or painting, and he makes plenty to support his car and to go have fun. No, it can't be James.

Tony doesn't have a job, that I know of. And he's always around the park somewhere. And he's always in trouble with something. Sweat runs down my back and down my face. My shirt makes a quick towel, as I keep moving on.

With the yard all mowed, front and back, I pause to water myself down with the garden hose. The cool relief from the heat, reminds me of the coolness of the reservoir. I can't wait until I'm in the water with my friends.

In the garage, I put up the mower and get out the trimmer. All gassed up and the trimmer string checked, it fires up with a few jerks. Around the trees and bushes I whack away. Along the landscaping, sidewalk and driveway. Time goes fairly quick. A few passes with the push broom along the sidewalk, I'm burning up. Ready to eat a snack lunch and get to the cliffs.

After a glass of lemonade and a peanut butter sandwich, I said, "See you later, Mom," and out the door again. Mom is shouting for me to be home by four o'clock. Three hours of fun will be long enough. I shout back to her, "Okay," as I pedal my bike to the street.

A distant lawn mower shuts off, allowing the katydids music to be heard across the quiet neighborhood.

Hardly no one is out in this heat, even neighbor dogs and cats who are usually out, are probably in the shade somewhere.

A few cars are driving by the park slowly, their license plate shows that they're not from this county. They must have heard about the cave in the news. But the heat is probably keeping people away as there are only a few down by the cave.

Up the cliff trail I pedal hard to reach the top. To the right side of the path, are The Buddies bicycles over on their sides.

Under the shade of the giant oak tree sits Jamie, looking out across the reservoir. Her long brown hair lightly being blown back by a slight breeze from the west. She didn't hear me riding up behind her, so I quietly get off of my bike and lay it down, without a sound. Tip toeing behind her, she turns just as I growl to scare her. "Lucas!" screams Jamie, "I've been waiting for you."

"Sorry, I had to trim and then eat some lunch," I reply, "Where are the others?" Down next to her, I drop to my knees.

"They're down cooling off," she said, pointing over the edge of the cliff. "I told them you'd be here soon, so I'd just wait for you." She gives me a smile that warms my heart.

"Thanks, that sounds good. Let's join them," I said, rising up on my feet. The rope hanging just in front of me, I hand it to her.

Then I check over the edge for clearance, Darwin and Stevie are over to the right, playing in the shallow water. "All is clear down below, Jamie."

She rears back and then runs off the edge, swinging out and dropping in feet first as usual. Her long hair seems to flow up to the sky as she screeches in the fall. She disappears in the waters with a splash. The rope swings back for me to grab, as I watch for her to come up.

Bubbles rise and then so does Jamie, clearing her nose, she waves up to me as Darwin and Stevie calls out in a cheer.

She swims over to them as I walk back to start my swing. Off the cliff I run and swing my legs to the timing of the swing. At the end, I kick up and flip a backwards double to land feet first. The waters feel so good as the coolness soothes my body. The Buddies all clap and whistle.

"Lucas, it's so hot we don't want to get out of the water," Stevie said, and splashing water at me. The three of them sit on submerged boulders up to their chins.

"Yeah, it's a scorcher out here," I reply, treading water close to them, "The water feels good."

We all sit in the shallows awhile and then Darwin went up to swing off of the rope. One after another, we took turns trying different jumps and flips. This fun day is one of many days we have spent going off of the cliff.

Even when I am 100 years old, I will never ever forget the good times we have spent here in this reservoir town. Simple and easy living, enjoying the hot summer days at the cliffs, cooling off in the waters with The Buddies. I can't think of a nicer time than doing this.

"Even when I'm 100 years old, I'll be going off the cliff in my wheelchair," Stevie said. We all busted out laughing.

An hour must have passed of us having fun, and when Stevie was up there to go off the cliff, Tony Watson peers over the edge. "Hey kiddies, the swim party is over. It's time for you to go, your Mommies are calling." We all look at each other in disgust and slowly get out of the water.

Jamie said, "Hope Stevie is all right," as she looks back to me and Darwin. Up the side of the cliff we climb.

"They wouldn't be that stupid to do anything to him," I said, as we were almost to the top. There to our far left is Stevie, on his bike about ready to leave, while watching us. Tony Watson wearing cut-off shorts, leaning on the rope, with a devilish grin. "Okay girls, you can all go now and we'll run this party now," Tony said. His two scum buddies stand by laughing.

We walk to our bikes and Jamie turns to speak up, "You jerks are so mean." Oh no, we're in big trouble now, as we start to pick up our bikes.

Tony's grin went flat, leaving the rope hanging and walks towards us. His two buddies are right behind him. We now have the look of fear and try to place our bikes between us and Tony Watson. Stevie who was already on his bike, takes off pedaling away fast. "No Tony," I said sternly. Tony's eyes are piercing right through Jamie.

"Apologize for that comment," Tony said in a bullish tone, pointing to Jamie and with his muscles tensed.

"You guys are mean jerks," she said, holding her bike out in front of her for protection.

"Tony, no," I said again and held out my right arm to halt Tonys progression. Tony pushes my arm away and reaches across Jamie's bike, pushing her backwards.

She falls back with her bike following her. This enrages me and without thinking, I push him back.

Tony falls over Darwin's bike and lays there staring at me, saying, "Now you've done it." Tony's buddies just stand there, like they couldn't believe what they've just seen. Tony jumps up and charges at me.

I run to where I have always felt most comfortable - the rope. But, one of Tony's buddies is in my way. The cruddy teen reaches out to grab me and so I gave him a straight arm, like I was running for a touchdown and knocked the teen back. But Tony is right on my heels, "Come here, punk," he snaps. His old tennis shoes tromping behind me.

A few yards ahead of me is the rope, which I knew I could safely reach. As I hang on and start my usual swing, Tony said, "No, you don't," and grabs my shoulders. But my speed and swing is strong enough to continue on as I lock my hands on for dear life.

Tony was so intent in catching me, he must have not been aware that we were both going off the cliff.

The rope holds both of us going off as I hang on with all my strength, but Tony's grip slips on my sweaty shoulders. His hands quickly slide down my back, clawing to get a grasp and almost takes my shorts off. My life-saving swing returns me to the cliff, as I watch Tony do a belly smacker in the shallows close to the boulders below.

The swing brings me safely back to the cliff, with Tony's buddies looking over the edge to see how he was. Darwin and Jamie are standing by with their hand over their mouths, probably fearing Tony's fall.

We all look down to see Tony was hanging on a boulder in the shallows, gasping his breath between painful yelps. His buddies glance at me and then run down to the right of the cliff, without saying a word.

"Tony, are you all right," I shout down to him. He didn't look up. He just moved slowly, hand over hand, along the boulders to the shallow right side. Moans and groans could be heard from him. His buddies climb out on the boulders to help him. One, asks him if he is okay. We could hear him say it was his left foot. He said he must have hit it on a rock.

We look again where Tony had fallen in the shallow water and with large boulders all around. His foot must have smacked one of them. "He's lucky to be alive," Darwin said. We all agree and feel his pain. His buddies are trying to help him out of the water, and Tony was painfully saying to wait, that he can get out on his own.

"Tony, do you want us to go get help for you?" I shout. His buddies glance up and talk among themselves. The Buddies look in fear for Tony, hoping he isn't too badly hurt.

One of the goons looks up and replies, "No, we're okay. Just go away." They slowly help Tony up on a boulder and carefully put his leg up on top.

His foot already looks swollen and black and blue. He is lucky that is all he got from that fall.

It could have been real bad.

"We better go as they had told us to," I said, as I get up on my feet.

"Do you think we should tell Officer Clifford about this?" Jamie asks, as we still watch Tony down below, trying to see how bad he is hurt.

"I don't know. It looks like a bad sprain and may be all right in a week or two. I've had a sprain before playing basketball and it takes time to recover," Darwin said.

"I don't think we need to bother Officer Clifford about this accident. Tony and his buddies probably has learned a lesson from this. Let's go on home," I said, turning away from the cliff edge. On our bikes, we coast on down the trail, only to see Stevie riding his bike back to us with Officer Clifford trotting at his side.

"Oh no, too late," Jamie said, glancing over at me. "What are we going to do now?"

"We'll have to tell what really happened. Which is the truth," I reply, watching them coming closer. The late afternoon heat now feels like it has cooled some to maybe ninety degrees.

"That's the best thing to do right now," Darwin said. We all apply our brakes to meet Stevie and Officer Clifford at the bottom of the trail.

"So glad to see that you guys are all right," Stevie said, with sighing relief.

"Hello friends, Stevie said there was a problem with Tony Watson and his bunch," Officer Clifford said, removing his sun glasses and glancing past us towards the cliff. He lightly pats my shoulder and looks at each of us for someone to start telling what had happen.

"Yes. There is a problem and we barely escaped with our lives," I said hesitantly.

Officer Clifford had us walk with him back up to the cliff, and explain what had happened. In the shade of the large oak tree, he had us rest, while he went down to check on Tony and his goons. Stevie peeks over the edge to see what was going. The rest of us just sit to try to stay cool. "What's going on, Stevie?" Darwin asks him.

"Officer Clifford is checking out his foot, and asking some questions," Stevie said.

"There won't be a problem, we didn't do anything wrong," Jamie said.

"Yeah, Tony and his buddies just need to be civilized, and leave everyone alone," I said.

"They're trying to stand Tony up on his feet," Stevie said, while stretching to see. "No... They set him back down and... Tony is crying in pain. Officer Clifford is now on his walkie talkie, while Tony's buddies try to calm him."

"Wow, is Officer Clifford calling for help? Like maybe an ambulance will come to get Tony," I said. We couldn't help but to crawl over to see what's going on. Officer Clifford is telling them something, but with the gentle breeze and the waves crashing, we can not hear what is being said. Then Officer Clifford leaves them and so we scramble back under the shade tree.

"Tony must really be hurt," Darwin said, drilling the ground with a twig.

As we sit here waiting for Officer Clifford, Jamie said, "It was a bad fall. He could have broken his neck."

"We all saw what had happened. I was just trying to get away from him," I said. The Buddies all agree and soon Officer Clifford climbs to the top where we are waiting.

"Tony seems to have a broken foot and so I have an ambulance coming for him," Officer Clifford said.

"They did confess to bullying you guys and so I'll have their parents come to the department later, so we can decide what to do about this problem they have," Officer Clifford said, wiping sweat off his forehead.

"I want to discuss a new discovery to you and your parents at the department this evening. It's a report we've all been waiting for and I want to tell you before it comes out in the paper tomorrow morning," He said with a smile.

We look up in awe, and I ask, "Yeah, What Time?"

"How about after supper, like seven o'clock?" He asks.

"Okay, we'll have our parents bring us," Darwin said.

"Good. Now you can go on home and don't worry about this. It will be resolved this time, as this has always been a problem with these guys," Officer Clifford said. We coast on our bikes down the trail. In the far distance, ambulance sirens can be heard. Like it was coming from Wabash, and is almost to the reservoir. Past the dugouts and up on the road we ride.

The sirens now sound close near down town, we turn to see the flashing lights coming up the street towards us. On the side walk, we park our bikes, straight up from the third base dugout.

We look across the ball diamond to the cliff trail. There standing on top of the cliff among the trees, is Officer Clifford, like he is waiting for the ambulance to appear at the park. As the ambulance pulls into the park entrance, Officer Clifford waves his arm, to get the attention of the ambulance driver.

We slowly walk our bikes along, as the ambulance drives on towards the cliff trail. Then it turns and backs up to the trail. Two men in uniforms jump out and with a first aid kit and a stretcher, then rush up the trail to Officer Clifford. All three of them disappear in the trees.

Now watching from the park entrance are a few neighbors, who must have heard the sirens. Even the visitors at the cave area, walk over to see what is going on. Not much can go on unnoticed in this town. Some nosey kids even ride their bikes past the ambulance and then run up the trail to see what's going on.

It was several minutes, when the kids came running back down the trail, announcing what they think is going on. Then soon right behind them was Officer Clifford, who is walking backwards down the trail.

He has one hand on the back of one of the ambulance guys, walking the stretcher down the trail slowly, with Tony Watson strapped on the stretcher.

Tony's buddies are helping steady the stretcher as the other ambulance guy is at the head. On Tony's leg was a brace, like he may have a broken leg, propped up on a pillow.

More people have come to the park to see what all the excitement was about. Some of the kids come riding past the ambulance, announcing "It's Tony Watson, he's got a broken a leg."

The ambulance now loaded and ready to leave, Officer Clifford tells the bystanders to make way for the ambulance. Up out of the park, the ambulance drives and heads north downtown, probably going to the hospital. Officer Clifford has Tony's buddies get in his squad car and then Officer Clifford drives away. "Is Officer Clifford taking them to jail?" Stevie asks.

"Not really. He's probably going to the station to have their parents come down to have a talk," I said.

"Yeah, like they did the last time, they were in trouble," said Darwin. And we all know they have been in trouble many times. Officer Clifford did say that this time was one time too many.

The Buddies rode on home, and will see each other at the station at seven o'clock with our parents. We would explain to them that there would be a special announcement made to only us. Then it would be published in tomorrow's morning paper.

Could the announcement be that the prime suspect has been found? Or maybe that the skeleton was identified?

Back at home, Mother was making supper and as I rush in the kitchen, I said, "Mom, we need to go to the police station tonight at seven o'clock for a special announcement."

Mother stops from layering a lasagna dish and turns to me, "What special announcement?" She asks.

"Officer Clifford told The Buddies at the park, to come to the station tonight at seven, with our parents for a special announcement."

"Is that all he said?" Mother asks.

"Yeah... No... In the morning paper, the announcement would be made public."

"So what do you think it could be?" Mother asks, as her hands drip tomato sauce, "Could it be who the prime suspect would be or who the mummy may be?"

"That's what we had thought too. Officer Clifford didn't say, just to be there at seven for the special announcement."

"Wow. This is going to be a big deal and being placed in the paper for everyone to know," she said and turns to work again on the lasagna. I wonder if Father will go with us as he is a possible suspect in this case. But then again, if he is not guilty as he himself would only know, then why wouldn't he go?

James comes home from mowing a yard and then Father drives in. They both go to get cleaned up for supper. The lasagna and garlic bread was wonderful. Our conversation around the table about the announcement were lengthily. Father and James each had their own thoughts about who the dark suspect may be and why. Neither one seems concerned.

They also had some ideas on who the mummy could be and some reasons about the bag of money. Some stories told are funny, especially the ones that James spoke of. Our Father being more reserved and quiet, unlike James.

Mother asks James if he would go with us to the announcement. James said, "No, I'm going to go play some basketball tonight over at David's house."

I didn't think anyone besides The Buddies and our parents would be allowed in the station for the announcement anyway. But James said he couldn't go anyway. He doesn't do much with our family ever since he got his drivers license.

"Is that your friend David Lowery, who lives over on east Monroe Street?" Mother asks James. Our Mothers friend is Mona Lowery, who is David's Mother.

"Yeah." James said, getting up from the table and hurries to the kitchen door, saying, "I'll see you guys later, around nine o'clock." Father turns to see the back of James rushing out.

Mother replies loud enough for him to hear her, "Be careful James and we'll see you around nine." Father finishes and then gets up to go get ready to go. Mother and I are left to clean off the table. Then we both go in our rooms to get ready ourselves.

On our way to the police station, while sitting in the back seat, I try not to visualize Father dressed in black hurrying from the cave. But driving by the park, in the dark shadows of the evening sun, a black ghostly image of Father disappears in the brush and trees. My imagination.

To Father I turn my attention to see him concentrating on his driving and not saying a word.

At the station, Darwin and his parents are going inside. We park behind Jamie's parents car and get out to go in. On the steps of the station, comes a familiar voice far behind us, "Hi Lucas." We turn to see Stevie and his parents walking towards the station. We wave to them and then step on inside.

A deputy sheriff asks us our names and then makes a check mark on a clipboard. Then ask us to go on into a conference room.

Inside the room is a large table with Officer Clifford, and another man whom we don't know, DNR Officer Asborn, a State Police Officer, Jamie and her parents and Darwin and his parents.

"Hello Lucas, Mr. and Mrs. Lousure. Please have a seat anywhere," Officer Clifford said.

Then Stevie and his parents then walk in and they were given the same welcome introduction. With everyone present and seated, Officer Clifford introduces everyone. The one man whom none of us knew, is Marcus Newbauer from the State Police Forensic lab. The State Police Officer introduced has been around this area many times.

Officer Clifford then explains, "Because The Buddies are the finders of this towns greatest discovery, we feel it is only proper to personally inform you, before it comes out in the morning paper, who the skeleton really is." The other Officers smile and nod their heads in agreement. The Buddies all smile back and look at each other with honor.

The State Police Officer dressed in his blues, said, "Twenty-seven years ago, the town bank was robbed. The robbery occurred over night, without any alarms or an obvious break-in. A local man who was a loner, lived up above the Laundromat, which is next door to the bank."

"The loaner's name is Thomas Wenzel. The State Police Lab identified the skeleton as being Thomas Wenzel, through a Wabash Dentistry where Thomas had to have a molar removed. He had no family around and only a few locals knew little about him."

Darwin's Father and my Father both gasp, and the State Officer said to them, "Do you remember Thomas Wenzel?"

They both look at each other and Darwin's Father said, "Yes. We were only like ten years old and he did odd jobs around town and kept to himself."

"That's right. Do you remember what happened to him?" The Officer asks.

"Something about he went down to the reservoir to go fishing one night and was never to be seen again," My Father said.

"Yes. Some of our interviewers, who knew him, said that he loved to fish at night for catfish. And that he took good care of his fishing equipment. It was believed that he had drowned because his fishing gear was found on the bank. One of the poles lines was stuck on a rock and the authorities believed he went in the water to unhook it. Never to come back."

"I remember the DNR trolled and searched the area, but couldn't find him," Darwin's Father said. My Father nods his finger and his head in remembrance.

"That's right. They thoroughly searched the reservoir with divers and could not locate him," Officer Asborn said.

"The police report on the bank robbery, read that Thomas was questioned and his apartment was searched. Thomas was found not to be related to the bank robbery. There was another possible suspect, but he too was found innocent. The case went cold and never came to light again," Officer Clifford explains.

"I do remember that, and we never heard any more about the robbery," My Father said, "And I also remember that a few kids had asked Thomas about it, and he said he knew nothing."

"Thomas must have led a private life and the reports we have, showed that he continued to do odd jobs around town, even though he had the bag of money," The State Police Officer said, "Thomas must have stumbled onto the cave and told no one about it. Its surprising that no one else had discovered until Lucas had found it."

"So from the investigation, officials have determined that Thomas would go to the cave where he had hid the money. Every so often, he would go into the cave to get a few bills. He was smart in the fact that he never showed he had a lot of money, just enough money or so from doing odd jobs. In his apartment, there weren't any signs of expensive or new articles like one who had money to spend," Officer Clifford said.

"Wow, that is something. So, what happened to Thomas?" Jamie's Mother asks.

The Lab Scientist spoke up to say, "There was no foul play. Laboratory tests showed high levels of a viral infection in his blood. Which was caused by the bat droppings over a long exposure time. Thomas must have stayed in the cave for long visits. Why? We don't know."

"He had a wool blanket with him to keep off the chill of the cave and he even covered himself and the money with a plastic sheet to shield the bat droppings," Officer Asborn said.

"So he would just come and go whenever he needed to and when it was safe," Father said.

"Yes. He must have been very careful about it," The State Police Officer said.

"Thomas did this for a few years after he robbed the bank?" My Mother asks.

"Yes, from 1941 when the bank was robbed, to the summer of 1946 when Thomas went fishing and disappeared," Officer Clifford said.

"So he set up his own missing-person death?" I ask, and everyone just looked at me, like a twelve-year old is not allowed to speak up.

"That could be right, Lucas. Or he must have known he was feeling ill and wanted to be with his money to the end. And took the secrets with him. Could be he didn't want to be prosecuted, fearing that the illness may lead authorities to the robbery," Officer Clifford said, "There are a lot of unknown possibilities for his secret."

Darwin spoke up, "Could it be that he got tired fishing and with it being pitch-black out at night, he just walked up the cliff to the cave to rest with his money. And then never woke up from his illness," he said, to our surprise as Darwin is normally quiet among people.

The State Police Officer said, "Yes, that is a good possibility. Or it could be a just a coincidence that he went fishing and went to get some money out of the cave, got tired and laid down to rest. And like you said, to never wake up again," The discussion soon left us to wonder.

"Ladies and Gentlemen, this is the special announcement we wanted to share with you. The story will be in the morning paper, for everyone to know the identity of the skeleton," Officer Clifford said.

I wanted to ask if they have any ideas as to who the dark suspect might be, but was afraid to ask with everyone there. We all walk out of the station, stone-face by the news meeting, all of us probably visualizing the whole story in our minds.

This leaves me to believe that the dark suspect is probably someone who may have also accidently stumbled across the cave, or someone who knew about Thomas's hidden secret and was keeping the secret to himself. Or maybe the suspect was his partner in crime.

CHAPTER SEVENTEEN

The Dark Secret Illuminated

As we sit around the kitchen table finishing breakfast, Mother reads the morning paper to us. The front page news sounds so shocking to James and I, as if I have never heard of this story before. Again this little country town will be rocking with the latest news.

"The news report explains the State Lab pathological findings of the autopsy, some money usage and a missing person from years ago." It was as if I were in a trance, drifting through a movie scene. "The lonely life style of Thomas Wenzle was sadly told. He was nice, but kept to himself and worked only to have food and a small apartment. His hobby was to go night fishing with fishing equipment he either had found or someone threw out." Our Mother reads on.

"The story goes on to tell about the cave he had found and how many people must have gone by the area without ever noticing it. And without seeing any bats around the hidden area."

"Some locals thought Thomas only had the IQ of a ten-year-old. But on the contrary, he was smart enough to somehow get into the bank and take about thirty-four thousand in cash. He was questioned, but was found innocent in the heist.

He then continued his daily life style, like he had done for the last twenty years, when he first walked into town."

"He had no family around that anyone knew of and maybe had a few friends in town. But no one ever became close to him, as he would shy away. Especially when some bullies made fun of him, as one local resident stated, but didn't want his name mentioned in the paper."

"Many local residents contributed information on Thomas Wenzel and kindly expressed their knowledge of him to the authorities. The State Lab had conducted tests on the corpse and concluded that Thomas died of a viral lung infection caused by long term exposure to the bat dung. This may explain the plastic sheet which covered Thomas and the money bag. He may have felt safe and comfortable with the money, spending time in the cave. So much time, he needed to cover himself with the plastic." Our Mother makes a gagging sound after reading that part.

"The article ended by saying most of the money had been returned to the bank, but about six thousand was unaccounted for. The investigation goes on, as several people are being questioned.

Finally, it says that a local boy, Lucas Lousure had accidently found the cave entrance in the town park this summer, and will be honored."

"The Department of Natural Resources had erected a secured memorial at the entrance of the cave. Mainly because a bat colony was discovered to live in the cave."

"DNR biologists had found it to be the Indiana Bat, which is rare, but not yet on the endangered list. So to ensure the species will thrive, they constructed a secure memorial site so the bats could continue to use the cave.

Again, thanks to our local hero, Lucas Lousure." Our Mother finishes reading the news article.

Mother slowly lowers the paper with a big smile on her face and a tear in her eyes as my heart pounds. The news article had brought Thomas Wenzel back to life. James looks at me and says, "Nice job, celebrity," and gets up from the table.

With a pat on my shoulder, he said, "I've got to go do a paint job for Mr. Duncan." And out the door he hurries away.

"He's all heart. Isn't he Mom?" I said, watching the garage screen door slam shut.

"James is a lot like his Father. Always working and not a warm heart," Mother said. "This news story shows the mystery of the skeleton and the story behind the bank heist and the cave."

"Yeah, it's a real good story and now we have a memorial monument in town."

"And the rare Indiana bats will thrive in their home, to come and go as they wish, thanks to you Lucas."

"Yeah, it all happened on an accidental finding." And that was no lie, I did accidently find the cave, but at twenty-five feet deep, down from the cliff. The Buddies secret to the end. "What bothers me now, is who the dark suspect might be."

"That's still a mystery. It could be someone just like Thomas, who needed money or also has a secret to keep. But we do know that the dark suspect didn't kill Thomas," Mother replies and glances down at the paper.

"Yeah, that's what the detectives said," as I get up from the table, "I'm going to walk down to the park to visit the memorial, Mom."

"All right. But be home in a few hours so we can go visit Grandma."

"Okay. See you in a few." The telephone rings and Mother get up to answer it.

"Hello," Mother says. As I stand at the front door, Mother has a strange look on her face. Slowly the look changes to a smile and she repeats "Yes," over and over again, while staring at me, "Thank you, that sounds wonderful. I'll call you back soon. Yes. Goodbye," She hangs up.

"What's going on?" I ask, just knowing something good is coming from that conversation.

"That was your Scout Master. He read the article and wants our permission to seek the town council to work on getting a day next year designated as 'In your honor' day, Lucas. Doesn't that sound wonderful? He wants us to talk about it and get back with him."

"Yeah... well... Okay, but I don't want the town to make a huge deal about this."

"Lucas, it will be a nice honor in your name. The town will be so proud of you."

"All right Mom, but I don't want a big whoopee doo event."

"Okay Lucas. I'll call him back and let him know."

"Thanks Mom. I'll be back soon." Out the front door I go, with my mind on the dark suspect.

Maybe they wanted to report the human skeleton finding to the police, but greed took over and decided to keep it a secret.

On towards the park, not really thinking about getting there, as my mind is on the dark motives. To my left came a startling running sound. I turn to see Darwin running towards me, "Lucas, where you going?" He asks.

With a deep breath, I said, "To the park." My mind still frazzled from being startled.

"Hey. Did you read the newspaper? That's a real good article." He puts his hand on my shoulder and that makes me smile.

"Yeah. It looked nice and sounded good, but it leaves me to think about the dark suspect."

"What about?" We walk on side by side almost to main street.

"What the dark suspect may have been thinking. Did he also want the money?"

"I was thinking the same thing and feel that someone knew Thomas. They knew his secret and maybe even was involved in the bank heist. The suspect also kept it a secret and when he or she needed money, would sneak inside to get some."

Darwin said softly to me, as we slowly walk closer to the park.

"Yeah, or it could just be someone like us, who accidently came across the..." From behind us came sounds of snarling, some bicycle chains clanging and screeching tires.

"Well, look at this." Tony Watson said, with his goons laughing at his side. Darwin and I jump up on the sidewalk to keep from being run into. We didn't say a word, but felt like trouble is here again. Tony is wearing a walking cast on his left foot. "Our small town hero. Someday your brother won't be around to protect you and the Long Ranger wont ride up to save the day." He must be meaning Officer Clifford.

Darwin and I stood still, looking at the black clothes all three of them wore. They're wearing sunglasses and their long greasy hair flipping around to their shoulders. "Tony... we have never caused you trouble..."

"Every time I see you, your trouble." Tony points his finger in my face. "Just watch your back, punk." They all start to peddle off, and then Tony stops, turns, and says, "Oh, and that cave," He points down into the park, towards the cave, "Belongs to us." They then all laugh and ride away, slipping into the neighborhood.

We could not believe what we just heard. We stood there and look at each with our mouths open. "What did he mean by that?" Darwin asks, with his arms out from his side in awe. "We need to report this to Officer Clifford."

"No, wait. You suppose they are involved in the cave and the money... or just harassing us?"

I reply and look across the street to where they disappeared into the neighborhood.

"It does seem very possible. But with all the news out and about, they could just be trying to get our goat." My buddy said. We look around and no one else is out on the streets right now.

"Out of all the suspects, maybe the detectives found the hoods to be prime suspects?"

"Don't know. But, they seem to be likely." Darwin replies. Down in the park, a Father is pitching baseballs to his son. We can hear him say, 'keep your eye on the ball and don't swing at any bad pitches.'

As we walk on to go on down the park, with another incident heavy on my shoulders, I said, "I can't believe we're still having problems with the goons. I thought for sure the last time was it for them."

The sun isn't as hot today as it had been and seems to be further to the south. Darwin said, "Yeah. I was hoping they would have been locked up in the detention home for a while. Don't you think Officer Clifford should know about this?"

"Probably, but I don't want this to go into war. And I didn't hear what came about on the last incident." We all were probably hoping they would have learned their lesson by now. We walk to the out field fence. There is no one at the memorial site.

"Lucas, I just feel that they're teenage bullies who like to push around kids younger than them."

"And we just happen to be in their neighborhood." Along the tree line we go, looking back to see if we're being followed.

"I hope it's just a faze and soon it will pass," I said, as we now stand at the gate of the cave. Just inside of the gate to the left about four feet is a post with a large memorial plaque on it.

The DNR plaque reads in large print;

The Indiana Department of Natural Resources has erected this memorial site in honor of the rare Indiana Bat who has a colony inside of this cavern.

The Indiana Bat is close to being on the endangered species list and it is important that they thrive undisturbed and remain protected.

On August the 4th, 1968, a local boy named, Lucas Lousure, discovered this cavern. Upon exploring inside, he found a human skeleton and other mysterious items, in which the investigation has solved a case which occurred twenty-seven years ago.

In honor and appreciation to Lucas Lousure, this memorial historical site is protected and preserved for the Indiana Bat and future generations to come.

"This is such an honor Lucas. I think this is the first time I've ever read it."

"Really? We were here right after they finished it. Remember when we..."

"Lucas!" Came shouts from above the park by the road. It was my Mother. "Come, we must get home to get cleaned up." I wave in reply as Darwin and I hurry along the fence row. I wonder what the hurry was all about, she knew I would be home soon.

Over by the dugouts, Mother drives up to us. "Lucas, get in, we must go. Darwin, can I give you a ride home?" Her hair messed up and her face looks flushed.

Darwin seems to sense something is up, says, "No thanks, I'm going to the cliff to walk around. See you later, Lucas."

"Okay Darwin, later," I said, as I get in the front seat. I close the door as Mother is already backing out, her face is now pale and clammy as she spins out of the parking lot.

"Mother! Is something wrong?"

"Lucas... We have to go get cleaned up... and get to the Police Department."

"What? What's going on?" I didn't understand the trouble and the big hurry.

"The detectives came to your Fathers work and took him to the Police Department. They called and asked us to come in for another interview."

"What do they want Dad for?" As we bounce in our drive and stop suddenly at our garage door.

"They said he is the prime suspect in the cave money heist."
Tears roll down her cheek.

As we both jump out of the car and run in the house, I said,
"Oh no!" Mother grabs some clean tissues to wipe her face. I
was afraid that Father may be, as he took those late evening
walks down by the reservoir. But why? Father has such a high-
paying job, that Mother doesn't need to work.

In the shower, I can't help to think why Father would. He
doesn't need the money. With my nice casual clothes on, Mother
shouts from the kitchen, "Are you about ready?"

"Yes. Combing my hair, I'm coming," I toss the comb on my
dresser and run out of my bedroom.

"I called Mr. Duncan's house to try to get hold of James.
Mr. Duncan said James is around somewhere, and he would tell
James as soon as he finds him. I told him where we would be."

"Do you think James would really care?" I said in a joking
reply.

"Lucas. Okay, let's go." Mother said, as we rush out the door.
In the car, she wipes another tear away. Soon we're zooming
down the road.

"Mother. I really can't see Father doing this. It just doesn't
add up."

"Yes, I know. It doesn't make any sense. He has no reason
to have been involved." At the downtown stop sign, there to my
right is Officer Clifford standing by. He waves, as I roll down
my window.

"Hello folks, what's the hurry?" He asks, shaking my hand.
Mother briefly explains the situation and wipes her eyes again.

I knew Officer Clifford would understand and gave Mother some encouraging words.

Before we could park the car, he also said that a friend of mine was attacked by Tony Watson and his two buddies, about half an hour ago.

They are in custody here and will be taken to the Wabash Detention home. He said the little guy is in good condition with a broken arm and was scared as they had held a knife to his throat.

"It wasn't Stevie, was it?" I interrupted saying.

"No. It was Barry Short," He said. Barry was a year younger and a friend in my school.

"Tony and his goons were on probation from a last incident. So this will place them in adult court and probably will be sentenced to a correctional facility for many years as habitual offenders and causing serious bodily injury. So this town will be safer now. I'll be around, if you ever need anything," Officer Clifford said.

"Thank you, we will be fine," Mother said. With our car parked in a spot, we jump out and rush to the station, as I sigh some relief to the news.

Inside the Police department, we're greeted by an officer, who directs us to a detective, then leads us to a conference room. He has us sit and offers us a bottle of water. The detective explains that the preliminary lab tests shows that Father's boots, coveralls and flashlight, had bat dung on them. None of the other ten suspects had bat dung on their personal possessions.

Mother sobs and dabs at her tears, and said she couldn't understand why he would do this.

I shook my head in disbelief, as it doesn't make sense.

The detective explains that even proper respectful people makes poor decisions and greed can make some do things, we normally wouldn't do. Sometimes it's the thrill of a bad decision that can move us in a wrong direction.

"What's going to happen next?" Asks Mother in a trembling voice. I look up to the detective to hopefully find some remorse.

"The bank whose money was taken, wants compensation and since it was a part of a bank heist, there will be a state trial.

In past cases similar to this one, I recall where one had received one to two years in jail and had to pay restitution."

"Oh no. No... no," Mother replies. I lean over to comfort her with my head down. A commotion in the front lobby occurs and a knock comes at the door. An officer peeks in and asks if my brother James can come on in to join us. My Mother replies, "Yes, let him in."

James rushes in and asks, "What's going on." Mother explains the findings and possible sentence to James. James doesn't say a thing and drops his head in his hands.

The detective pulls a chair up next to Mother for James and also adds some explanation as to why.

I believe this is the first time I have ever seen James cry. "So... Father could even lose his job?" James asks and gets a nod from Mother. "When can we see our Father?"

"Soon, in a while. They're processing him now to be transported to the Wabash facility," the detective replies.

The stress and repeat discussions, with what-ifs, is too much for me. "Mother, can I please go for a walk? I need some fresh air, please Mom." I held her hand, seeking my plea.

"Where are you going, Lucas?" She asks with red weeping eyes.

"I don't know, just to the cliffs to get some fresh air and to think," I said.

"All right. Just be careful, Lucas. We'll be home in a little while." James doesn't look up from hiding his face.

Once outside, I run as fast as I could, up the hill towards the park. Tears roll by my ears, soaking my wind blown hair.

A car honks at me, but I don't look or even wave, full flat out speed with my heart pounding, is doing me good right now. Down into the park, I race on. To my left are some kids, but I don't see who it is and don't care. My name being called out, is faintly heard, but there is only one thing on my mind.

Up the cliff trail, I struggle on. This exercise does me good, as my mind relaxes some and the fresh air coming up from the reservoir fills my lungs. Now at the cliff, there is one last thing I need to do.

Full speed again, the hanging rope is in sight. As if I was running for the finish line in first place, I grab the rope and run right off of the cliff. Out across the reservoir, I swing high and in a split-second, glance to see if it was clear down below. It was, and so I let go!

As if I was in slow motion, I flew out like a free bird. Out stretched arms and legs, wanting to gain as much air as possible.

Didn't even care that I was wearing nice clothes or my good tennis shoes. The cool reservoir water awaits my thirsty stressed body.

It seems like I flew for a few minutes as I point straight into the refreshing waters. Oh! What relief the freshwater gives me. I just relax and let the diving speed take its course. This is the soothing medicine I need right now.

Slowly I come back up to breath again, turning to swim back to shore. Mother is going to be upset about my clothes and shoes, but they will dry. For a second, I thought about diving on down to go up into the cave. But a voice in my brain quickly told me, 'NO, Lucas.'

On a large boulder I rest for a few seconds and then climb on out. Up the side trail I slowly climb, my soaked shoes slipping with each step. At the top of the cliff, I sit under the large oak tree to look out across the reservoir. My life feels crushed right now.

The steady breeze helps to dry me off. Sun rays break through the canopy of tree leaves to help shed some light on me.

"Did you enjoy the swim?" Came a familiar voice from behind me, as I turn to see Jamie. She is standing there with her arms crossed.

Beside her is Stevie and Darwin, staring at me as if I had lost my mind. A pool of water drains away from my soaked clothes. "Hello Buddies. You want to join me?"

They sit down next to me, avoiding the wetness. Jamie gently moves some hair out of my eyes. "Darwin told me something was up. You want to talk to us?" Her smile melts my heart and her eyes must see right through me.

All along in our friendship, I must have been fooling myself. Jamie has been good to me, so she must be my girlfriend. I now admit to it and with all that is now said, makes me smile, and surprisingly, I feel a lot better.

"Yes. I need to tell my Buddies something," I said, and just to let it all out. From the Tony goons up until now, The Buddies sit and listen. Stevie for the first time in his life sits still, he didn't fidget or interrupt, just listened to my problems. I was amazed. He must be growing up.

Darwin pats my shoulder, showing that its all right. He understood. The whole story was told

and complete, now they suspect my Father to be the dark suspect. Father had said before he didn't really know Thomas Wenzel. He said Thomas was a loner and a few made fun of him.

The Buddies sit in awe, not asking a single question. I quietly said, "So right now, all we can do now is wait."

Jamie takes my hand and says, "This is hard to believe, Lucas." She must mean my Father being the dark suspect. All I could do is nod my head in agreement or I would probably lose it.

Stevie rubs my knee and said, "Lucas, we are all Buddies to the end. We can talk about anything." I had to close my eyes on that one, and reach out to hug all of them. "Ugh. You're all wet." We all giggle. From the cliff trail, we could hear foot steps tromping up towards us.

We all look up to see Officer Clifford walking up, saying, "Hi Buddies, Mrs. Lousure said I could find you here. I should have known."

We all said, "Hello." But I wonder what's up now? A visit from an Officer here, is not just to say hello.

"Lucas, your Mother wanted me to find you, for me to tell you about the latest news. Its not as bad as it was, but still bad. Can I tell you in front of your friends, or privately one-on-one?"

Without hesitation, I said, "Right here is fine. These are my Buddies. " And with that said, Officer Clifford, plops right down on the dusty ground in his uniform and crosses his legs, Indian style. Jamie is to his left, I am in front of him, Stevie to my right and Darwin to my left.

"All right. Well, It was soon after you left the station, when your brother James had heard enough. The scenario of your Father being put away for several years and losing his job, was too much. James confessed to the crime." Our mouths all drop open. "Yes. And he wasn't just trying to cover up for your Father either. James said he was playing ball one day several years ago in the park. A home run ball was hit over the fence and while getting the ball, he noticed the dark entrance through the vines and roots. He didn't say anything to anyone about it." Officer Clifford said, then went on to explain.

"Later that evening, he got a flashlight to explore it. He put on your Father's old muddy boots, not wanting to get his boots muddy and went exploring. Found the skeleton and the money bag, just as you did this summer."

"He didn't bother the skeleton, but temptation got a hold of him. He took a bill, later on, took another and later on, a few more bills. He said even though he had a job mowing yards and painting, it wasn't enough to support his car and to have fun."

"Many times he would say he had a job to do, when actually he didn't. He would just play it up, to keep his secret a secret." The Buddies all sit still, as I hang my head in disbelief.

"He didn't think anyone would know anything about it, being hidden in a cave. The money looked old and he didn't think it would matter." The Buddies just listened and shook their heads in disbelief. "He said he knew it was wrong and he wanted to report it, but greed had him.

He really thought he would never be caught. He said he was very careful not to be noticed.

A few bills here and there, with all of that money, what would it matter if he took some?"

I put my hand over my eyes, in disgust for James. I was relieved that Father is innocent of any charges. "Lucas. It is hard to believe, but for your families sake, your Father is innocent and now free to go. No harm done." Officer Clifford gives me a gentle rub on my shoulder.

"James spoke of his dark secret twenty-five feet inside the cave. He talked about how he would never ever tell anyone. But... the terrible fact that your Father would probably go away for a few years, really broke him down. The talk about him losing his job and probably the home, tearing the family apart. That's what really hit home. It's probably hard for you to see through his thick hide, but deep inside, he does have a heart." Officer Clifford explains it so well, we all seem to understand.

"What's going to happen to James?" I ask, as my Buddies follow my eyes to Officer Clifford, probably wondering the same thing.

"Being a minor of sixteen and the fact that no-one knows how much money Thomas had spent, and how much James had spent, this will go to the juvenile court."

"He may have to pay some restitution to the bank and may have to be on house arrest. I really don't know," He said.

"Where is James now?" I ask. The Buddies all look up to Officer Clifford for an answer.

"He is with your Mother and Father in conference with the detectives, and will soon be taken to the Wabash Juvenile Detention Center. Until lawyers can sort this all out and decide on the next juvenile court date."

The Buddies all seem calm with the latest news, as we readjust our sitting positions. Officer Clifford slowly gets up with some grunts, and says, "Wow, I guess I'm not as young as I use to be, " as he rubs his bottom, "Are you all right, Lucas, with the latest news?"

We all get up and I reply, "Yeah. Your right, the news isn't as bad as Father's news first was."

"It's still not good when someone in our family does something wrong. We have to pay for our bad decisions. Hopefully, good citizenship prevails. I need to get going, if you have any questions, get with me. Can I give you kids a ride home?" He asks, while brushing off his pants.

The Buddies all said we were fine and are just going to hang out here. "Okay, see you guys around town. Take care." He turns and walks away, still brushing off the back of his pants.

"Wow! This day is so heavy on me," I said, slowly running my fingers through my hair. My clothes are just damp now, as Stevie brushes some debris off my pants.

"Lucas, if it's any relief to you. Many issues were resolved today and tomorrow will be a brighter day," Darwin said. I look at him and smile, as he is exactly right.

Jamie wraps her hand around my hand and says, "You have faced many tasks, Lucas. From diving down and exploring a cave, to working off a debt with James and then dealing with Tony, and finally all of the press and investigating process. You are a special person and we love you." She reaches up and gives me a kiss on my cheek. Stevie holding on the tree rope, giggles as we finish with a gentle hug.

With the sun hanging above the western horizon, I said to The Buddies, "Thank you Buddies, for being my Buddy. You know I couldn't have done it without you. We've been friends for years and we will always help each other out."

The Buddies all congratulated each other with pats on the back and handshakes. In the calmness of the summer late afternoon, The Buddies stood together and then sat on the edge of the cliff, I quietly said, "The Buddies dark secret at twenty-five feet deep is our secret for life." I know that someday, we will revisit the underwater cavern.

THE END